Award-winning *USA TODAY* bestselling author **Yvonne Lindsay** has always preferred the stories in her head to the real world. Married to her blind-date sweetheart and with two adult children, she spends her days crafting the stories of her heart. In her spare time she can be found with her nose firmly in someone else's book.

TANGLED
WITH A TEXAN

YVONNE LINDSAY

MILLS & BOON

First Published in Great Britain 2019
by Mills & Boon, an imprint of HarperCollins*Publishers*
1 London Bridge Street, London, SE1 9GF

© 2019 Harlequin Books S.A.

ISBN: 978-0-263-08096-4

MIX
Paper from
responsible sources
FSC® C007454

This book is produced from independently certified FSC™ paper
to ensure responsible forest management.
For more information visit www.harpercollins.co.uk/green.

Printed and bound in Great Britain
by CPI Group (UK) Ltd, Croydon, CR0 4YY

To my fellow Texas Cattleman's Club: Houston authors, always a pleasure working with you, ladies!

One

As if it wasn't enough she'd had to hand over her additional casework to the rest of her already overloaded team, now she was headed all the way out to Royal, Texas. Zoe Warren was a city detective, hell, city girl, through and through. She already could start to feel her skin itch at the thought of cattle and cowboys and all that open pasture. Mind you, driving the three hundred or so miles to Royal had presented as a far more attractive option than facing yet another blind date set up by one of her four older brothers or her parents, who seemed to think she needed help settling down. And who said she wanted to settle down, anyway? She'd worked long and hard for her place on Houston P.D.'s detective squad, and her career trajectory was heading straight up. You weren't a third generation cop without some dreams and goals ahead of you—and at only thirty years old, she had plenty of dreams and goals to fulfill while quite happily still single.

Sure, one day it might be nice to get married, throw a couple more Warren genes into the pool of rapidly growing family her brothers and cousins were constantly adding to. But not right now. And not on her ever-loving family's timetable, either.

The open country that surrounded her had a raw beauty to it that even her citified eyes couldn't help but appreciate. But always, in the back of her mind, she was working. As lead detective on the homicide case that was sending her on this journey, she was beginning to feel like the more they uncovered about the deceased, Vincent Hamm, the less they actually knew about him, and for her, following down each and every rabbit hole in Hamm's life had become an obsession. The good thing about having this time on her own as she drove west toward Maverick County was that it gave her the opportunity for some thinking time. Time without the constant pressures that came with the responsibilities of her job.

Everything about this case was off. First, the vic had disappeared into thin air, then he'd never shown back up for work, and after the floodwaters had receded at the site of the new Texas Cattleman's Club being built in Houston, he was eventually found dead with his face destroyed. Whoever killed him had taken great pains to ensure he couldn't be visually identified—although the floodwaters had taken their toll, too.

Zoe took a swig of her water bottle and grunted in annoyance when she found it empty. Still, not long now and she'd be in Royal—she could stock up at a convenience store there. But first, a quick swing by the sheriff's office was in order to make a courtesy visit and let them know that she'd arrived in the county. Nathan Battle, the sheriff, had made a personal visit to Houston to lend his support to the case. Her vic was the son of a friend of his and she'd expected Battle to be loudmouthed at the very least, and difficult at worst. Instead, she'd been quietly surprised by his demeanor. Oh, there was no mistaking the determination behind his promise to Hamm's family to get to the root of who murdered their son, but he was a by-the-rules guy and his help here in Royal could prove invaluable to her investigation. She'd gone to great lengths to ensure she was doing everything in her power to bring the murderer to justice, and she was confident she'd earned the older man's trust. She liked the guy. Not pushy, just determined. She respected that.

About ten minutes later, guided by the GPS on her phone—without which she'd be totally lost anywhere, not having inherited the direction gene her brothers took for granted—Zoe pulled up outside the Royal sheriff's office. Three minutes after that she was back in her car. Turned out the good sheriff was out on a call, but she'd left a message for him to phone her when he got back.

She reprogrammed the GPS and found the midrange motel she'd booked just on the other side of town. It didn't take more than ten minutes to check in and unpack. She called for updates from her colleagues back in Houston and let them know she'd arrived safely, then decided to take a short walk around town to stretch her legs and familiarize herself.

Royal struck her as a prosperous town with a decent-sized population scurrying about their daily business. Being late afternoon, there were all kinds of people out and about. Business people, moms and kids, a handful of idlers loitering here and there, but overall the place had a good feel about it. She turned and headed back to the motel, her mind still churning over the facts of the case. Just as she reached her unit, her phone buzzed in her pocket. She slipped it out and looked at the screen. Nathan Battle.

"Sheriff, thanks for calling," Zoe answered.

"Thanks for coming by and letting me know you're in town. Did you want to meet?"

"How about tomorrow afternoon?" she suggested, mentally reviewing her plans for tomorrow morning, which included following up on the lead that had brought her to Royal in the first place.

She heard the flick of paper, followed by a grunt of assent. "Yup, works for me. I'll meet you at the Royal Diner for coffee and a slice of pie, say, three o'clock?"

Zoe's stomach growled in response to the mention of food. "Sounds like a plan. See you then."

That would give her plenty of time to make the drive out to the Stevens ranch in the morning and ask a few questions. Hopefully more than a few. That cryptic message left on Hamm's answering machine saying no more than "Thanks for nothing, Hamm" had spoken volumes when taking into account the tone of the speaker and the fact that Vincent Hamm had gone missing around the same time. They'd been able to trace the message to a local rancher, Jesse Stevens. Research had shown Stevens and Hamm had been friends at one time, but what had happened to drive them apart? Had it been enough to make Jesse Stevens want to kill his former friend?

Stevens was quite a force here in Royal. The wealthy rancher was very involved in the politics of the local Texas Cattleman's Club, and while Zoe may be grasping at straws, the fact that her vic had been found in the building currently being developed into a new Cattleman's Club might not be such a coincidence after all. Right now, she had to look at everything. Pressure from the chief of police and Houston's mayor was constant, and so far her team had little to show for their investigation. Her captain had pulled her aside just yesterday and asked her if she was getting stale. The question had made her bristle. Stale? When all she did lately was live, eat, sleep and breathe this case? Not likely. But he'd made it clear—he needed to see results or she might be stood down.

Thinking about it, Zoe reached a decision. She didn't want to wait until morning to go face-to-face with Stevens. She could drive out to his ranch right now. October sunset wasn't until around seven, which gave her three hours of daylight. Plus, the element of surprise would be in her favor if she just rolled up without an appointment. She opened her map app on her phone and pulled up the address she'd saved for Stevens's ranch before leaving Houston. The ranch was outside Royal and isolated. Nothing but pasture and cattle. Zoe ignored the itch between her shoulder blades and got into her car, set her phone in the hands-free holder and hit Start on the journey planner.

The drive took longer than she expected, but as she pulled through the gates of Stevens's ranch she felt a sense of triumphant relief that she had made it. People could tease her all they liked about her reliance on modern technology to get anywhere, but it got the job done, she thought with a small smile.

She was still smiling when she went up the front stairs of the impressive ranch house and knocked on the front door. But her smile slipped when no one came to answer. She knocked again and waited a couple of minutes before walking along the front porch to one of the side windows. She looked in. No movement, nothing. Zoe blew out a huff of frustration. Maybe a phone call would have been a better idea after all. Still, she had a list of his known associates here in Royal and she knew one of them was his neighbor. She walked back to the car and reprogrammed her app to the next address on her list.

This time she struck gold when she knocked at the door

of the neighboring ranch, which was no less impressive in size and structure than the Stevens property. She'd always known ranching was a prosperous undertaking when done right, but the two properties she'd been on so far were something else. She plastered a smile on her face and flicked her short dark hair back off her forehead as the steady sound of footsteps coming to the door echoed from the other side.

The words she was about to say dried on the tip of her tongue as the door opened, revealing a tall, imposing presence. While the guy wasn't heavily muscled, there was no doubting the latent strength in the shoulders that bunched beneath the checkered shirt he wore over a crisp white T-shirt. Zoe's gaze flicked up—something she wasn't always used to doing when wearing boots that, combined with her natural height, put her at around six feet. Instantly, her attention was captured by the man's eyes. Light brown and shot with gold, they were incredibly mesmerizing and were set in a face that was all sharp lines and angles softened by a generous dusting of five o'clock shadow that wrapped his jaw. There was an almost wolflike look to him—as if he were assessing her as prey.

Rather than getting put on the defensive, Zoe found herself reacting on a far more visceral level—each facet of her mind sharpening, while every cell in her body responded with pure feminine interest. A wave of physical need pulled from deep within her, robbing her of breath and making her nipples harden against the lacy cups of her bra. She drew her full lower lip between her teeth to stop herself from making the involuntary sound—something like a moan—that threatened to spill from her.

The man's hair was wet, as if he'd recently stepped from a shower and just slicked it back—its wet ends kissed the edge of his collar and left a damp trail. She drew in a sharp breath, only to discover how intoxicating the scent of him was. She was shocked at how deeply and suddenly he had affected her. She had trained herself from day one at the police academy not to show her emotions. Good things, bad things—it made no difference. She had learned to remain impassive, detached. But right now, she was anything but detached. In fact, right now, every instinct was screaming at her oversensitized body to plaster itself against his length and take his mouth in a possessive kiss that would leave him in no doubt of how much she wanted him. For a nanosecond she allowed herself the luxury of imagining where that might lead. To their two bodies, glistening with perspiration, tangled in tumbled sheets, gliding together, perhaps? She blinked hard and forced herself under control. This was utter madness. She couldn't even remember the last time she'd reacted to a guy this intensely.

Those intriguing eyes narrowed as he looked at her, and she realized that neither of them had spoken.

"Miss? Can I help you?"

His voice poured over her. Deep and strong and sexy as hell. This guy could recite a list of traffic infringements and make her knees turn to water.

"Detective," she corrected him, showing him her badge. "Zoe Warren, Houston P.D."

"You're a little out of your jurisdiction, aren't you?"

She wasn't mistaken. The warmth and pure male interest she'd seen reflected in his eyes had dimmed, his gaze sharpening warily.

"The boundaries of our investigation have stretched a little," she said carefully. "I'd like to ask you a few questions, Mister...?"

"Cord Galicia," he answered abruptly and thrust out his hand.

Zoe debated taking it. If her reaction to him on a purely

visual basis had been so extreme, how on earth would she react when she actually touched him? There was only one way to find out. She drew in a sharp breath, took the proffered hand and clasped it. A slow sizzle of awareness tracked along her skin. His hand was larger than hers, the palm firm, and she could feel the calluses that spoke of the hard work he did. The title of rancher wasn't simply some token. This man clearly worked, and worked hard. Did he apply himself to everything else he did with as much vigor? she wondered before giving his hand a quick shake and releasing it.

"May I come in?" she asked.

To her surprise, her voice remained steady. Quite a feat when her insides were jangling about as hard as they had in junior high when she'd been asked to prom by the captain of the soccer team. She was already head and shoulders taller than him but it hadn't bothered her—until she found out the whole thing had been a joke designed by the rest of the team. But that initial response, the delicious sense of anticipation and excitement, she'd never forget. She just never expected to feel it here on the outskirts of Royal, Texas, while working a homicide investigation.

For a moment it looked as if he'd refuse, but then he stepped back from the doorway and gestured for her to move inside. He closed the door decisively behind her, but Zoe didn't let it rattle her. She'd dealt with people with far fewer social graces than Cord Galicia.

"Can I get you anything to drink?" he asked as he led the way into a large open-plan living room.

"Water would be great, thanks."

"Take a seat," he said gruffly before heading through a doorway toward what was, presumably, the kitchen.

Zoe sank into a large leather sofa. In a smaller room the piece of furniture would have dominated, but not here. She looked around, taking in the high raftered ceiling—must be a bitch to keep clean, she pondered—and the tall windows that led to a paved courtyard outside. Large round ceramic pots in a jumble of bright colors, some with mosaics, were filled with flowers, and beyond that Zoe caught a glimpse of the sparkle of late-afternoon sunlight on water. A pool or an ornamental pond? she wondered.

"Here you are."

Cord Galicia stood before her holding a sweating tall glass of water in one hand. She reached up to take it.

"Thank you."

The man moved with the stealth of a wild animal, she realized. There weren't many who could sneak up on her like that.

"You said you had questions," he said as he settled onto the other end of the sofa.

"Yes, I do. Your neighbor, Jesse Stevens—are you well acquainted?"

She knew the men were best friends, but she was curious to see how Galicia reacted to being questioned. She kept her eyes focused on her host and didn't miss the way his body stiffened.

"What do you want with Jesse?"

"Please, Mr. Galicia, just answer the question."

"He's my neighbor, of course we're acquainted," Cord said begrudgingly. "But I don't see what he has to do with some investigation in Houston."

"That's my job," Zoe said with a grim smile. "Tell me, what's Mr. Stevens like as a man?"

"What do you mean?"

"Is he quick to anger? The type to follow up on a grudge?"

"I don't like where you're heading with this. Jesse is a decent man and an upstanding member of our community. If you're looking at him, you're looking in the wrong direction."

Zoe decided to take a different tack. "Do you remember Vincent Hamm?"

"Yeah, he grew up around here. We all did."

"Were he and Mr. Stevens particularly close?"

Cord shook his head. "No, I wouldn't say that. Jesse knew him, sure. But we all did. Is that who this is about? Hamm? Look, we were sorry to hear he'd passed, but it's not like we'll miss him. Seriously, we haven't moved in the same circles for years. Like I said, if you're after Jesse, you're after the wrong person. He's the most law-abiding and stand-up person I know."

"You'll forgive me if I don't immediately jump to believe you. That's pretty much what everyone says when asked about the people they think they know."

Two

"*Think* they know?" Cord didn't bother to keep the irritation out of his voice. "Since I've known the man most of my life, I can safely say I know Jesse Stevens pretty damn well, Ms. Warren."

"Zoe, please."

Oh, so she was attempting to play nice now? He let his gaze drift over her. He wouldn't have minded playing nice with her, if she'd been anything but a cop. She was exactly his type. Long and lean with sweet curves in just the right places. Even her short-cropped dark hair was sexy, and he bet it looked even sexier mussed up against a crisp white cotton-covered pillow. He shifted slightly in his seat as his body reacted in ways his mind was determined not to.

"The fact remains, I know my friend, *Zoe*," he said with emphasis. "And you're barking up the wrong tree."

She dragged in a deep breath, and he couldn't help but notice how her fitted shirt strained against the buttons across her chest. Oh yes, sweet curves all right. But off-limits, as was any woman serving in the police force. Cord let his gaze drift to the photo frame sitting on the antique sideboard across the room. Britney. God. Seeing her graduation picture from the police academy every day was a reminder of everything he'd lost. Her death two years ago, while on her first shift of active duty, had been soul destroying, and it was Jesse who'd kept him sane through that awful, dark time.

No, Jesse was not the kind of man to commit murder, and Cord would do whatever he could to ensure Detective Warren knew that. And, he reminded himself as he flicked his gaze back to the woman in front of him, if he ever embarked on a long-term relationship again, it wouldn't be with a woman who wore a badge and a gun and hunted down bad guys for a living. No matter how much his libido told him otherwise.

"Sometimes we're not always honest with the people we're closest to," she said in an obvious attempt to placate him. "Do you know when would be a good time for me to catch Mr. Stevens at home? I called on him earlier and no one was in."

"He runs a working ranch, so I guess it's safe to say there's never a good time. We have to make the most of the daylight hours available to us," Cord said, hedging, unwilling to give the woman more information than was absolutely necessary.

"Well, I caught you at home, didn't I? Mr. Galicia, are you being deliberately obstructive or is this just your charming way of treating all strangers?"

"Obstructive?" Cord felt a trickle of irritation at her insinuation. He wasn't being obstructive; he was being careful. They were two very different things.

"That's the usual terminology when someone deliberately withholds information."

He watched as she picked up her water glass and drained it. Her throat was long and slender, the muscles working delicately as she swallowed her drink. Damn if the sight of that pale column of skin didn't give him a hard-on. She snapped the glass back onto the table in front of her and rose on those enticingly long legs, then reached into her back pocket for a business card. She handed it to him as he hastened to stand.

"Call me if you suddenly remember how I can best reach Mr. Stevens," she said with a slight curl of her lip. "I'll be staying in Royal for a few days."

"Does the sheriff know you're in town?"

He could see she wanted to tell him that was none of his business, but instead she gave him a brusque nod.

"Of course," she said. "He's assisting in my inquiries."

Cord nodded. That made sense. The sheriff and the Hamm family went way back. "Maybe he can tell you how to get ahold of Jesse, since he's assisting you and all."

He couldn't resist goading her just a little. It rankled that she'd come out here without any notice on some jumped-up idea that Jesse was involved in Vincent Hamm's murder. The very thought was ridiculous. Jesse was the kind of guy to always bend over backward to help others, and Cord knew he'd gone the extra mile with Hamm on several occasions. And then the one time Jesse had to ask Hamm for a favor...

A frisson of warning prickled at the back of his mind. Was that what this was about? Had this woman unearthed something about Jesse asking Hamm a favor? A favor Hamm had refused to act on. Was that her angle? That Jesse had somehow been mad enough to exact revenge?

"I'm sure he will. Next time I talk to him, I'll be certain to get the lowdown on you, too."

"Me? Hey, you want to know about me, feel free to ask me anything." Cord spread his arms wide and quirked one corner of his lips up in a smile. "I'm an open book."

She sniffed. "Thank you for the water. No doubt I'll be speaking to you again."

The thought of seeing her again had its merits, but he doubted she meant what he was thinking.

"I'll look forward to it," he replied, imbuing into that handful of words enough innuendo to make Ms. Warren stiffen and give him a hard look.

"We'll see about that."

He led the way to the front door and watched her as she stepped onto the porch. There was a determined set to her shoulders, and he knew she wouldn't be deterred by him. One way or another she'd track Jesse down, and Cord didn't want it to be today. Jesse had enough on his plate with his sister's emergency surgery today. It had started out as routine to remove an inflamed appendix, but the dang thing had already ruptured, spilling infection through Janet's body. While she was receiving the best care possible, Jesse was beside himself with worry. Last thing Jesse needed was this detective visiting him in the hospital.

Maybe Cord could appeal to her good will, he thought. Just as the woman reached her grime-covered car, he called out.

"Jesse is at the hospital—that's why he's not at home right now. His sister had an operation today. There were complications. He's been there all day. A decent person would leave him be."

"Mr. Galicia, are you suggesting I'm not a decent person?" She cocked one brow as she raised the question.

"Well, that remains to be seen, doesn't it?" he challenged. "Give him a couple of days at least."

"And what do you suggest I do in the meantime? Paint my nails?"

He had to hand it to her. She didn't back down, not one bit. He probably shouldn't have told her about Jesse being at the hospital, but he'd hoped he could appeal to her sense of compassion. Surely she had one in there somewhere behind that blue-eyed deadpan stare of hers?

"Maybe we could have a drink or a meal somewhere?"

"Are you asking me on a date?"

The incredulity on her face would have been funny if it hadn't been so insulting.

"Sure, why not?"

For a second or two she looked totally at a loss for words. As a distraction tactic, asking her out clearly had merit, he thought with a quiet twinge of satisfaction. At least it appeared to have stopped her in her stride.

"What about it?" he pressed. "Tonight, just a drink. You can ask me anything you want."

"I can ask you anything I want anytime I want. I have a badge, remember?"

"What? Are you afraid of spending time with me?"

She snorted. "I'm not afraid of anything, Mr. Galicia. Especially not you. Sure, fine. What time and where?"

"Why don't I pick you up? Where're you staying?"

She named the motel.

"How about seven?" he asked, beginning to wonder what in hell he was letting himself in for.

"Seven is good."

Then, without another word, she got into her car and swung it around the circular driveway and back toward the main road. Cord watched until she went out of sight, then slowly closed the door to his house. His grandmother would have said he'd gone totally loco. Even he didn't understand fully what had prompted him to make the offer to Detective Warren, aside from the need to protect his best friend from her questioning. He flicked a look at his watch. Jesse said he'd be at the hospital until the nurses kicked him out. It would take the detective about forty minutes to get to town from here, then no doubt she'd want to fluff a bit like women did. She wouldn't have time to go to the hospital and bother Jesse, but just in case, Cord dragged his cell phone from his back pocket and thumbed a text to his friend.

How's Janet doing?

She's holding her own. They're talking about removing the breathing tube later tonight.

Cord felt a pang for his friend. Janet was the only family he had left, and to say he was protective of his younger sibling was an understatement. This hiccup with what should have been a routine procedure today had surely devastated him.

Good to hear. BTW, Houston detective in town asking questions about Hamm. I'm taking her out for a drink so she doesn't bother you.

Jesse's reply was swift.

LOL, taking one for the team? Such hardship. Is she pretty?

Trust his friend to ask the hard questions.

Yeah.

But she's a cop.

Yeah.

Do you know what you're doing?

Keeping her away from you, remember.

There was a pause, and Cord began to wonder if that was an end to their conversation, but then his phone pinged again.

Are you sure that's all?

You know my rules.

Okay. Don't do anything dumb.

As if. Hey, give Janet my love.

Will do. And let me know how your date goes.

It's not a date.

She's pretty. It's a date.

Cord rolled his eyes before texting his reply.

She's a cop. It's not a date. End of story.

He pocketed his phone and went to his room to get ready to head into town. But even as he changed into a good pair of jeans and a fitted shirt and splashed on a little cologne, he couldn't help but wonder why he was going to so much effort for the woman. Was it because he was trying to keep her distracted and away from Jesse, or was there something more? He snagged his car keys in one hand and headed toward the garage. There was only one way to find out.

Three

Zoe paced the confines of her motel room, wondering why the hell she'd agreed to this—whatever this was—with Cord Galicia. The man exuded pheromones like body odor. Both were equally unwelcome in her book. Galicia had been far too cagey about Stevens, and her own experience had shown that people don't generally hide something that doesn't need to be hidden. And even though he had said she could ask him anything she wanted, she doubted that would extend to more information about his neighbor.

She flicked a glance at the digital clock next to the bed. He'd be here any minute. As if she'd conjured him up merely by thinking about him, there was a firm knock at her door. She swung around and checked the peephole. Yup, just as sexy as the first time, she thought. She forced herself to take a deep, steadying breath before unlatching the chain and opening the door.

Even with the distance of a couple of hours, he still

packed the same punch. She'd never met a man before who had made her feel so darn feminine. She wanted to say she didn't like it, but there was something about the way the blood in her veins fizzed when he was around that she had to admit wasn't entirely unpleasant.

"Good evening," Galicia said, then bowed with a flourish. "Your chariot awaits."

"We're not walking?" she asked, stepping through the door and carefully locking it behind her.

"Nah, the place I'm taking you is on the other side of town."

"If you'd have said, I'd have met you there."

"What's the matter, Detective? Don't you trust me?"

She snorted. "I can handle you."

He gave her a sharp look that made her draw in a hasty breath. It was clear his mind had gone straight below the waist. Come to think of it, so had hers. Instead of giving in to the sudden roar of heat that flamed from deep inside her, she narrowed her gaze at him.

"Well, where's this chariot?"

He laughed, the sound a deep rumble that hit straight to her solar plexus. A delicious, lazy sound better suited to a bedroom than a parking lot beside a B-grade motel.

"Over here."

He gestured toward a classic F-150, and as they drew nearer, he opened the passenger door for her. She eyed the antique surface of the truck. Clearly left to go to rack and ruin at some point, the vehicle had been restored, but the paintwork remained aged and patchy—almost as if the rust was a badge of honor.

"Ranching not going so well?" she asked, casting an obvious eye over the multicolored hood.

"Let's just say I appreciate the patina of time. It's been

treated and clear coated. A testament to the age and longevity of the beast."

Zoe cast him a sideways glance. A somewhat romantic statement from a man who made his living from the land and the animals upon it. Eschewing further comment, she climbed up onto the front seat and waited while he closed her door and stepped around to the driver's side. The cab had seemed so spacious until he swung up beside her. Then his shoulders were suddenly too close to hers and the cologne he wore wove around her on subtle waves of body heat. She turned her head to the window, but it was no good. Her senses were powerfully attuned to him. She didn't need to see him to know that his leather jacket was so soft and worn that it fitted his shoulders like a second skin, or that the crisp denim of his jeans pulled across his hips when he sat at the wheel.

She also knew that no matter where she was, she'd never again smell that scent and not think of him. Of the raw masculinity he exuded in his simple stance, or the latent power in his hands, the teasing in his eyes, the sardonic curl of his lip. She gave herself a mental shake. What the hell was she doing, thinking of him in these terms? Right now, he was someone of interest in her inquiries. Someone to question, not drool over. She was not that weak nor that vulnerable.

But it had been a while since she'd been intimate with anyone, and, she reminded herself bluntly, a woman had needs. Needs, it seemed, that were hell-bent on distracting her from her job. Well, she owed it to her victim to get to the bottom of who was behind his murder—and to bring them to justice.

They hadn't driven long before Galicia pulled up the truck outside a small hotel.

"This is us," he said, getting out of the truck and walking around to her side.

To preempt him opening her door, she did it herself and dropped down onto the pavement. She'd keep her distance from him, get whatever information she needed and then she'd be on her way. She didn't want to stay here in Royal any longer than necessary. It might be a thriving town, it might even be civilized, but it wasn't her city. These weren't her people. Especially not the tall, commanding figure walking beside her as they entered the hotel and headed toward the bar.

If she wasn't mistaken, there was a brief flare of approval in his eyes. Not that she cared. She wasn't here to impress him. He gave her a brief nod and put a hand at the small of her back, guiding her toward the bar. As they entered, he gestured to one side of the room.

"We'll sit over there."

She noted he made it a gentle order, not a suggestion. Okay, so he thought he was in charge. It was his turf. She'd play his game. For now.

"What's your poison?" Galicia asked as they reached their seats. "No, wait, let me guess."

She played along, watching as he stroked his chin and eyed her thoughtfully.

"Something frilly to counteract the tough-cop act."

"I assure you, it's no act—and you'd be wrong. I'll have a beer."

She couldn't help but notice the attention paid to him by the waitress who hurried over to take their order, but aside from a polite "thanks," he paid the woman no heed. Instead, he kept his searing focus very firmly on Zoe. The waitress was back in a moment, two chilled glasses and two ice-cold longneck lagers on her tray. She set the drinks onto the table in front of them.

"So, Cord, did you want these on your tab or—" the waitress started.

"I'll take care of them," Zoe said, flicking some bills from her pocket and dropping them onto the woman's tray. "Keep the change."

The waitress looked from Cord to Zoe and back again, Obviously she wasn't used to Cord's dates picking up the tab. She left as Cord picked up a beer, poured it into Zoe's glass and did the same for himself.

"You're quick," Cord said with a quirk of his lips. "I appreciate it. Thank you."

"I pay my way."

"Gender equality and all that?"

"You drove, I bought the first round. Gender equality has nothing to do with it." She arched a brow at him as he chuckled softly. "Are you deliberately trying to irritate me? Because if so, you'll find I'm hard to put off."

"I'm definitely not trying to put you off."

He smiled again, the movement of his lips sending a sucker punch to her gut. How did he manage to have such a strong effect on her? This was crazy. She'd been out with plenty of men, had relationships with a few, but she'd never felt this intense, visceral response before. It made her feel vulnerable, as if she were cast slightly adrift, and she didn't like it one bit. Determined to maintain the upper hand, she took charge of the conversation.

"So, how long have you lived around Royal?" she asked.

"Ah, the inquisition continues," he drawled. He sat back in his chair, hooking one arm over the back, and gazed at her through narrowed eyes.

"Inquisition?"

"Yeah, it's what you do, isn't it? Grill people?"

"Like dressed in black leather with torture implements and stuff like that?"

His lips quirked again, sending a spiral of sensation curling through her lower body. Oh, that mouth. How would it feel against hers? How would he taste?

"I could see you in that getup."

She snorted a laugh. "In your dreams, buster. So, back to my question. How long have you lived here?"

His nostrils flared on an indrawn breath. "Am I wet off the back of the truck, do you mean?"

She rolled her eyes. He was needling her, twisting her words to sound like a veiled insult. That might be the angle some of her colleagues would have taken, given there was no mistaking Galicia's Mexican heritage. But she was not that kind of person. In fact, none of her family was.

"Look, I asked you a simple question. You're being deliberately evasive again." She lifted her glass and took a long sip of her beer, relishing the bite of hoppy flavor as it rolled over her tongue and down her throat. "I'm not sure what you call conversation in this neck of Texas, but where I come from, when we meet a person, we chat, ask questions. Y'know, get to know one another."

He nodded slowly. "We have similar customs here."

She fought back a laugh. "I wouldn't have guessed it. Maybe it'd help if I went first? I'm Houston born and raised. Youngest of five. Third-generation cop. Your turn."

"Royal born and raised. Only child. My grandparents came here, bought land, ranched it, expanded the ranch. My father took over, did more of the same."

She nodded. "And you? Still expanding?"

He shrugged. "Not in land, more in better ways to use it."

She sat back in her chair and felt herself relax as he began to open up and discuss a little of how he planned to diversify his business operations. She let his voice roll over her, enjoying the timbre and the slow, measured way in which he spoke. She gestured to the waitress for two more beers.

"Let me get those," he said.

"If you insist," she acceded.

Once the drinks were on their table, she decided to turn the conversation back to her investigation.

"So, you and Jesse Stevens. You guys grew up together?"

"Yeah. And he's not the man you're looking for."

Ha, so much for softening him up and then pouncing with a question, Zoe admitted to herself with a measure of reluctance. Cord Galicia may have relaxed with her, but it didn't mean his mind wasn't as alert as a fox's.

"Why are you protecting him?"

"Protecting him?" Cord laughed. "Nope, I'm just saving you time."

"You realize I have to question him."

"Why? Is my word not good enough?" Galicia challenged her.

She saw the latent anger that simmered beneath the surface. Was it because she wanted to question his friend, or because she was impugning his honor by not accepting his word?

"I'm sure your word is just fine." She sighed. "But that's not how we conduct an investigation."

Silence stretched between them, and for a moment Zoe thought the evening was over. She felt a pang of regret. If she'd met this man under any other circumstances, then maybe they could have explored this simmering attraction that burned between them. She watched Galicia's face carefully, but he gave nothing away. Eventually, he leaned forward and put his hand out.

"How about a truce, then?" he suggested.

"A truce? I didn't know we were at war."

"Oh, we're at something, but I'm not quite sure what it is yet. How about, while we find out, we agree that you won't ask me anything about Jesse and then I won't need to stonewall you?"

She hesitated a moment before taking his hand. If she did this, she was opening herself up for a whole lot of trouble. She could feel it in her gut. But then again, what was life if it meant not taking risks? She reached out her hand and felt a surge of awareness the moment their palms touched. He felt it, too; she could see it in his eyes. He wasn't smiling now; in fact, he looked serious—serious about her.

Her inner muscles clenched on a wave of pure lust. Right now, she wanted to do nothing more than lean across their table, sweep their drinks aside and reach for him, then drag his face to hers and plant her lips on his mouth in a deep, drugging kiss that would hopefully assuage some of this crazy pent-up tension he manifested in her.

Instead, she jerked her hand free and reached for her beer, downing half of it. When she looked back at Galicia, amusement reflected back at her in his gaze and she knew, in that instant, he was dangerous. Maybe not in the criminal sense of the word, but certainly in terms of her equilibrium.

She was a long, tall streak of trouble. He knew that as surely as he knew the head count of his herd. But he couldn't leave her alone. Even now, after that stupid handshake, he wanted to touch her again—and not just her hand. He wanted to see if those pert breasts he could see pushing against the fabric of her shirt would fit neatly into the palms of his hands. He wanted to trace the cord of her throat with his lips and his tongue, to taste her and inhale the very essence of her.

Damn, but she did things to him that twisted his gut in knots without even trying. Which meant he had to be doubly careful. He was breaking every single one of his own rules by taking her out tonight. Still, it wasn't as if he was going to marry her or anything dumb like that, he told himself. He was distracting her. Keeping her away from Jesse. She had no business with his friend, and the sooner she realized that and returned to Houston, the sooner he could get back to his normal life. Thank goodness things were a little quieter on the ranch right now. The calves had been dried out and had regained condition. His pastures were under control and his hands were onto the usual maintenance required before winter set in. He had time to spare and he'd make sure he used it well.

"Say, you want to grab a burger or something?" Cord asked before finishing off his beer.

"I could eat a burger," Zoe admitted.

"C'mon, the Royal Diner makes the best burgers in the state."

"That's quite a claim," she said, rising from her seat.

"It's no claim. It's a fact," he boasted.

Putting his hand at the small of her back again, he guided her to the door. He liked the way she moved, all smooth and lithe, her gait a match for his own. His mind flashed in an instant to how they would move together—on a dance floor, between the sheets of his extra wide bed. Damn if he didn't get a hard-on. He reminded himself that this wasn't just about him. This was about keeping Zoe Warren away from his best friend.

Cord knew Jesse had been in touch with Hamm before Hamm's tragic death. He also knew Jesse had been fired up about the guy. If Zoe figured that out, she'd likely put two and two together and make whatever the hell she wanted out of it. There was no way Jesse had killed Hamm. He might have been mad at the guy, but violence had never been Jesse's style, not even when truly provoked.

They reached the truck, and he held her door for her. She brushed by so close he could smell the scent of her shampoo or whatever it was she'd used in her hair. It made him want to lean in and inhale more deeply. To touch her short black hair and see if he could tangle his fingers in it as he brought her face to his. He must have made a sound, because Zoe stopped midway getting into the truck.

"You okay?" she asked.

"Never better."

"Hmm."

She swung up, giving him an all-too-brief glimpse of her sweet butt showcased in dark denim. He closed the door firmly and went around to his side, all the while wondering what on earth he'd let himself in for.

Four

The woman had an appetite, Cord observed admiringly as she tucked into a double beef burger with all the trimmings. He'd ordered the same for himself. He nodded at a few of the people he knew as they went by, but mostly his attention was on the woman seated opposite him in the booth.

"Nice place, even better food," Zoe said when she finished her first bite.

"It's a staple here in Royal. You're always guaranteed a good meal."

"I like it. Thanks for bringing me here."

The simple compliment with her thanks made him feel ridiculously proud.

"So, tell me more about yourself," he said. "You mentioned you're the youngest of five? Is that right?"

"Yeah. I like to tell everyone that my mom and dad tried five times before they got the mixture right. My brothers would disagree. If they ever listened to me, that is."

Cord smiled. "Wow, four brothers. I can't even begin to imagine what that was like growing up."

As an only child whose future running the family spread was clearly outlined from birth, he had often wondered what it would have been like to share the load with one or more siblings. But from what he'd seen with a lot of his peers, siblings were overrated. Zoe spent the rest of their meal regaling him with stories of the things her brothers got up to while trying to keep her in line. Emphasis on the word *trying*. Seems she'd been a handful as a kid, and Cord wouldn't mind betting she hadn't changed much.

They were lingering over coffee when he saw her fight back a yawn. It made him realize the time—nearly ten. While that wasn't late, when you'd done a five-hour drive, like she had, or in his case, been up since before the crack of dawn, it was definitely time to bring the evening to an end.

"It's getting late. I'd best get you to your bed."

His choice of words had color flaming in her cheeks. He felt an answering wave of heat pulse through his body, too. To distract them both, he signaled for the check and paid, without demur from his guest this time, and they went out to the truck. When they reached her motel, he got down from the truck and walked her to her door.

"Thank you for dinner," Zoe said after opening her motel room and flicking on the light. "I enjoyed the company. It can get lonely on trips like this."

"Happy to help you pass the time," he drawled in response.

Even though he'd chosen his words to tease, oddly, he meant it. He'd engineered tonight to keep her away from Jesse but found himself enjoying her company. Hell, if he was totally honest, enjoying her. The air grew thick and heavy between them as she looked up into his eyes. Without thinking, Cord raised one hand and slid it around the back of her neck as he lowered his face to hers and gave in to the impulse to see if she tasted as good as he'd been imagining all evening.

He felt the shock that rippled through her body as his fingers touched the bare skin at her nape. Felt the sense of hesitation before her lips parted and she kissed him back. He'd been wrong. She tasted far better than he could ever have imagined, and somewhere along the line their kiss went from a questing beginning to something hot and hard and hungry. It was as if they were combustible elements, drawn together into a conflagration that took them both by surprise.

Zoe made a sound, like a deep hum, and he was lost. He wanted her—all of her. Forget she was a cop, forget she was investigating his best friend and most likely him, as well. Forget everything but the sweet, spicy flavor of her mouth, the softness of her lips and the urgency that pulled them together.

He snaked one arm around her waist, hauling her to him. Being tall, she lined up against his body perfectly, her hips against his, her mound pressing on his erection. She rolled her hips, and he groaned involuntarily. The subtle pressure of her body against his was driving him to the brink of his control. If this was what she could do to him clothed, imagine what they could do to each other naked.

Her hands slid over his shoulders; her fingers clenched on the leather of his jacket as he deepened the kiss. When his tongue tasted hers, she shuddered from head to foot. He did it again. Ah yes, there was that little hum from deep in her throat. She wasn't a passive woman. She gave back as good as he'd given. Her tongue was now dueling with his. And then she was pulling him through the doorway. Together they shuffled over the threshold. He kicked the

motel room door closed behind them and spun her to push
her up against the door.

Lacing his fingers with hers, he lifted her hands up so
they were against the door on either side of her head. Then
he bent and kissed a hot trail of wet sucking kisses from
her lips to her finely boned jawline and down the sweet
cords of her neck. Beneath his touch he felt her heated skin
jump as sensation transferred from his touch to her. He let
go of one of her hands and cupped her breast through her
shirt, groaning in frustration as he felt the pebbled nipple
against his palm.

This wasn't enough. He needed to touch her properly,
without the barrier of clothing. His hand was at her buttons before he knew he'd even formed the thought clearly.
In his haste he realized he'd torn one button loose from
her shirt entirely when he heard the faint sound as it hit
the carpet at their feet. But even that couldn't stop him in
his pursuit of the need to see her naked. The front of her
shirt fell open and he tugged the tails from her waistband
and shoved the fabric aside.

He sucked in a sharp breath. She wore a black lace bra
under that almost-masculine shirt of hers. The woman was
a total contradiction. Touch-me-not plain clothing and lingerie made for sin beneath it.

"What do you think you're doing?" she asked, her
breathing ragged.

"What does it look like I'm doing, Detective? I'm undertaking an investigation of my own," he growled.

He reached to cup one of her breasts in his large hand.
Yeah, she fit like she was made for him. Rubbing his thumb
across her distended nipple, he leaned in and buried his
face against her skin and inhaled deeply.

"You smell so good. I could lose myself in you, Zoe
Warren. Fair warning."

The hand he'd freed stroked down the front of his body until she cupped his erection through his jeans. "Looks like I have something to scrutinize here, myself."

He flexed against her, enjoying her boldness. "You gotta do what you gotta do, right?" he chuckled.

The sound strangled in his throat as she tightened her grip on him. She wasn't shy, but then neither was he. He gently tugged down the lacy cup of her bra, exposing her breast to his mouth. Taking her nipple carefully between his teeth, he rolled the nub with his tongue. Zoe's head fell back against the door and she moaned. Letting her other hand go, he reached behind her back to loosen the hooks of her bra. He was still impeded by the straps remaining over her shoulders, but at least now he could shove the enticing garment up, exposing both her breasts to his starving gaze.

Her nipples were a dark raspberry pink, topping luscious creamy skin. He kissed one, then the other, his hands cupping her from underneath as he divided his attention between them. Zoe had let go of him, her fingers now knotted in his hair, holding him to her as if she never wanted to let go. That was fine by him, he decided as he let one hand drop to the fastening of her jeans. He swiftly undid the button and pushed down her zipper before reaching inside.

He felt the heat of her before he even reached the damp lace at the juncture of her thighs. It was a tight fit, his large hand inside her jeans, but it was worth the discomfort to feel how hot she was for him, how ready. His own arousal grew to painful proportions as he touched her through the lace, pressed on that spot that made her cry out in pleasure.

He took her mouth again in a deep, intoxicating kiss, his tongue probing her mouth in time to the pressure of his fingers on her down below. She pressed into him, as if she couldn't get close enough, and then, in a sudden rush of heat, he felt her climax against his hand.

It took every ounce of control not to come in his jeans as she shuddered beneath his touch. Instead, he used his caresses to gentle her, as he would one of his horses, with slow sweeps of his hands—drawing out her pleasure, prolonging his own torture. He knew it would take only a moment to unfasten his jeans, sheath himself and drive into her heat right here against the motel room door. But when he made love to her properly—and he knew he would sometime, hopefully very soon—it would be in a large comfortable bed where he could truly explore what they could achieve together.

Cord straightened her clothing and kissed her again.

"I'd better go."

"Go?"

For the first time since he'd met her, she sounded unsure.

"Yeah, I'll be seeing you soon."

With that, he moved her bodily away from the door and opened it. He strode straight to his truck and got immediately inside, no mean feat when he had a hard-on that made his jeans uncomfortably tight as he settled himself into the drive home. He hazarded just one look at the motel room door before he backed out of the parking space. She stood there, holding the front of her shirt together with a bemused expression on her face.

Good, let her be bemused. While he might be in agony and his balls might be blue, he'd left with the upper hand. Let her think on that for a while.

Zoe rose the next morning still mad. She should never have let him kiss her, let alone touch her like that. And she'd climaxed, right there against the motel room door, she thought, staring balefully at the unassuming slab of wood. She never came like that—so quick, so intense.

Even now, thinking about it, she felt a tingle of anticipation all over again. Damn Cord Galicia for being so clever with his hands. *And don't forget his lips and tongue*, her subconscious oh-so-helpfully supplied.

This was hopeless. She needed to get out of here and do something, anything, to replace the memories Cord had instilled in her last night. She wondered how he'd felt as he'd left—whether he'd taken care of himself later once he'd gotten home. Perhaps in the shower, with hot water coursing over his body like a lover's caress. It was all too easy to picture in her mind and all too distracting, again.

She strode angrily to the bathroom. It was basic but, like the rest of the motel room, clean and functional. Besides, with how uptight she was feeling right now, there was no way she was going for comfort. Setting the shower to as cold as she could bear, she got under the spray and pulled the curtain across to encapsulate herself in the small space. She lathered up quickly and rinsed off, skimming her body with her hands and determinedly pushing back the memories of another set of hands on her pale skin. Of broad suntanned fingers touching and teasing her body, of those same fingers coaxing responses from her that had left her limp and sated and hungry for more at the same time.

It angered her that she'd been that easy. She'd come to Royal to further her investigation, not to have meltingly hot sex against a motel room door. And what was with that? Where had all her good sense gone? She'd been the one to drag him across the threshold and into her room. And when he kissed her, she kissed him back, as if she'd been starving for that level of attention. Okay, so maybe that bit was true, she admitted ruefully as she snapped off the shower and reached for her towel. It had been a while, and she'd never been the type to enjoy casual encounters. Her work made maintaining a relationship difficult at the

best of times. She worked long hours, dedicated to both
her team and to the victims whose stories she had to un-
cover. And that was what she was here for, she reminded
herself sternly as she wiped her still-tingling body dry.
Work, not play.

By the time she was dressed, she realized she was starving. She'd spied a coffee shop when she'd driven into town
yesterday. It might be a good place for her to formulate
her plan of attack for today. She still needed to get ahold
of Jesse Stevens and actually talk to the man. She got into
her car and, using the hands-free kit, called the number she
had for the Stevens ranch. This time she got a staff member, but she still wasn't able to speak to Jesse. Frustrated,
Zoe drove to the coffee shop.

She got a parking space right out front and walked up to
the café, laughing under her breath at the name, the Daily
Grind. Her nostrils were assailed with the delicious aroma
of freshly roasted coffee beans the moment she entered.
She ordered her coffee and a Danish and took a seat looking out the front window. Royal was a busy place, she realized, as people headed on their daily commute to work
and school. The Daily Grind was no less busy as people
stopped in for their morning coffee on their way to work,
or settled in for a quick breakfast. When her coffee and
Danish came, she took her time enjoying the flavors and
skimmed the news on her phone. It looked like the Houston papers were still bemoaning the lack of progress in
the Hamm murder.

She knew it wasn't personal—they had little to go on,
but even so it irked her intensely that they hadn't been able
to discover more by now. A heading regarding the Texas
Cattleman's Club caught her eye. It looked like the official
opening would be going ahead next month. No doubt that
would be a glittering affair with all of Houston's who's

who of anything important in attendance. She wondered about the guy who'd featured as an early suspect in the Hamm case—Sterling Perry. A leading contender for the presidency of the new club, he was an arrogant piece of work who wore his family's wealth like a second skin. She would have loved to have seen his ass nailed when her colleagues had arrested him on suspicion of operating a Ponzi scheme, but he'd been cleared of that. Even when he'd been suspected of being involved in Hamm's murder there'd been nothing to support the initial leads—the guy was like Teflon. Nothing stuck.

And then there was the other guy vying for the presidential role, Ryder Currin. Younger than Sterling Perry, Currin was far more charismatic and her research had shown he'd come into most of his money through sheer, hard work. Even now, despite his millions, the guy dressed as if he'd just stepped off the ranch. Zoe had wondered if the rivalry between the men had anything to do with Hamm's murder, but Ryder Currin had an airtight alibi for the window of time when Hamm was murdered. He'd been stranded at a local shelter when the storm hit and Angela Perry, Sterling Perry's daughter, had been there, too, and had vouched for him.

Zoe consumed her Danish and knocked back her coffee before leaving a tip and returning to her car. Maybe she'd have better luck tracking Stevens down at the hospital. Cord had told her his sister was there.

The Royal Memorial Hospital was easy to find, and visitor parking was relatively empty at this early hour. No doubt because visiting hours weren't until later in the day, she realized. She clipped her badge onto her waistband and went inside, knowing that the badge might give her access she would otherwise not get.

Sure enough, she was shown through to a ward where

Janet Stevens was recovering. The young woman was in a room on her own—apparently having been moved there not long before, after a brief stint in ICU post surgery. That was obviously why Cord had been so protective of his friend, knowing the other man must have been worried about his sibling. Galicia's protectiveness was, at its heart, an admirable trait, except for the part where he'd attempted to stall her investigation.

It made her wonder anew if that incident between them last night hadn't just been a distraction tactic. Something to blur her mind and keep her off Stevens's trail. Maybe he'd thought the little woman would be so blown away by what he'd done to her that she'd even hightail it back home.

Zoe discarded the thought almost as quickly as it bloomed in her mind. She'd been the one to pull him into her room, not the other way around. If anything, she was to blame for what had happened between them. And he'd been the one to walk away, unfulfilled. What did that say about the man? She shook her head. He was a conundrum, that was for sure. One she wouldn't have minded exploring further, if the circumstances had been different. But they weren't, and she had a job to do.

Zoe presented her badge to the duty nurse and asked if she could have a few words with Janet Stevens. The nurse was cagey, but after a quick call to Janet's doctor she said that Zoe was allowed five minutes, no more. Grateful for that, Zoe entered the younger woman's room.

Janet Stevens was pale but breathing without assistance. Walking farther into the room, Zoe watched the other woman as she opened her eyes.

"Good morning, Ms. Stevens. How are you feeling today?"

"Okay, I guess."

Janet's voice was groggy, as if she was still on some heavy-duty pain relief.

"I won't take much of your time," Zoe said quickly and introduced herself, explaining why she was there. "I'm sorry to bother you, but I can't seem to get ahold of your brother. I need to ask him a few questions."

"About Vincent? Whatever for? I know Jesse was mad at him, but he would never have hurt him," Janet protested.

"Can you tell me why your brother was mad at Mr. Hamm?" Zoe pressed, feeling a surge of excitement that she might finally be getting closer to finding some of the answers she needed.

"It's all my fault," Janet said weakly. "Jesse asked Vincent if he could return a favor and find me an internship at Perry Holdings. I've completed my MBA and Jesse thought Vincent would be decent about helping me. Turns out that while he was happy to accept Jesse's help plenty of times, he wasn't so keen to return the favor."

Would that have been enough to make Jesse Stevens commit murder? People killed over less. And it depended on the level of help Stevens had extended to Hamm in the past and what he thought the dead man owed him. She needed to meet the man to gauge for herself. A sound at the door had her looking up. Seemed she'd be meeting Jesse Stevens sooner rather than later, judging by the thunderous appearance on the face of the man entering the room.

"Who the hell are you and what are you doing in my sister's room?" he growled.

He was tall, blond like the girl in the bed beside her and he had piercing green eyes that looked as if they could cut through steel. His sister lifted a hand.

"Jesse, please," she implored gently.

"Detective Zoe Warren, Houston P.D.," Zoe said, gesturing to her badge on her waistband. "And you are?"

Even though she knew exactly who he was, it was important to her to establish who was in control.

"Jesse Stevens."

He answered bluntly, without offering his hand. It seemed she was persona non grata. A tiny smile curled her lips. Good, she liked knowing she'd riled him from the outset. Holding the upper hand was always her chosen starting point.

"Ah, Mr. Stevens. I've been trying to get ahold of you. Didn't you get my messages?"

A faint flush of color marked his cheeks. "I did."

She maintained her silence while raising one brow at him. His flush deepened. Just then, the nurse who'd directed Zoe to Janet's room appeared in the door and gave Zoe a stern look.

"Ms. Stevens needs to rest," she said pointedly.

"Thank you, I'm just leaving. Mr. Stevens, can I have a word with you outside?" Zoe asked.

"One minute, that's all."

Well, we'll see about that, Zoe thought to herself as she preceded him into the hallway outside his sister's room.

"Is there somewhere we could speak privately?" Zoe asked the nurse.

The woman gestured to a small sitting room down the hallway.

"C'mon," Zoe said to Stevens. "The sooner we get started, the sooner you can get back to your sister."

Realizing he had no reason to object, he fell into step behind her. Once they were in the room, Zoe closed the door behind him.

"What do you want?" Jesse asked, his voice and stance both belligerent.

"Just need to ask you a few questions."

"Ever heard of email?"

Zoe snorted lightly. "It's a strange thing," she said slowly. "We cops prefer to do things face-to-face. You can learn a lot about a person that way. So, tell me, why have you been avoiding me? Got something to hide?"

Anger flashed in his eyes for a moment before he visibly dragged himself under control.

"I have nothing to hide. What's this about?"

"Vincent Hamm." She threw the name into the conversation as if it were a gauntlet thrown in challenge.

"I knew him. What about it?"

"Been in touch with him lately?" she probed.

His gaze grew flat and cold. "Not for a few months. Why?"

"And when was the last time you spoke with him?"

"To be honest with you, I haven't spoken to him in a long time." Stevens huffed out a breath and rubbed his cheeks with one long-fingered hand.

Zoe grabbed her notebook out of her jacket pocket and flipped through a few pages before citing a date from a couple of months ago.

"Does that date sound familiar?"

"No more than any other date," Stevens replied.

"What about this—*Thanks for nothing, Hamm.* Do you remember saying that?"

"That's what this is about? A phone message?"

"Answer the question, please."

"Yeah, I remember saying that."

"You sounded pretty pissed off."

"Look, it isn't what you're thinking."

"And what am I thinking, Mr. Stevens?"

"How the hell would I know? You're a cop. It's bound to be bad, right?"

"Mr. Hamm is dead. I want to know how he came to be that way."

Stevens, to his credit, looked stunned. "You think I did it?"

"I'm not sure what to think right now," Zoe said honestly. "But you're not helping your case by being evasive with me. Let me warn you, Mr. Stevens. I am very good at my job, and I will get to the bottom of this."

"Look, it wasn't me. I wasn't anywhere near Houston when he was killed."

"So, you know exactly when he was killed?" she asked pointedly.

"Of course I don't. Look, whatever happened to him, I had no part of it. In fact, I was at a stock auction, buying cattle. I've even got receipts to prove it."

"Perhaps you would like to inform me what part you do have in my investigation during a formal interview to which you can bring those receipts."

Stevens rubbed his face again. "Sure, when?"

"Let me talk to Sheriff Battle. I'll work something out with him and I'll be in touch. And this time…?"

"Yeah?"

"Answer your damn phone."

Five

Cord's phone chimed to signal an incoming message. It was from Jesse.

Met your new girlfriend today.

Cord tapped the icon that would ring Jesse's phone. Texting was all well and good but sometimes you just needed to talk. This was definitely one of those times. His friend answered on the second ring.

"Is Janet doing okay now?" Cord asked.

No matter how mad he was right now, certain things needed to be taken care of first.

"Yeah, surprisingly well, considering how sick she was straight after surgery. They moved her onto the ward this morning before I got there. Gave me a heart attack to get up to ICU and find she wasn't there."

"I bet."

After Jesse and Janet's parents died, the two of them became even closer, since all they had left was each other. Cord could only imagine how Jesse must have felt to find Janet missing from the room where she'd been taken after surgery.

"I was surprised to see your girlfriend had beaten me there, though."

"I don't have a girlfriend," he enunciated carefully.

Even so, he knew exactly who Jesse was talking about, and the slow burn of fury rose from deep within. She hadn't listened to a word he'd said. Not only had she not stayed away from Jesse, she'd gone to the hospital and bothered Janet while she was at it. He rode the wave of anger for a few long seconds. Jesse was talking, but the buzz in Cord's ears made him sound like he was some distance away. Eventually Jesse's words sank in.

"She's a mighty fine-looking woman, even if she is a pain in the ass. Had some questions for me and wouldn't leave until she'd asked them."

"She questioned you? There at the hospital?"

She had nerve, he'd give her that.

"Yup, and I've agreed to an interview at the sheriff's office, too."

"You don't need to do that." Cord bristled. "And if you do, make sure you take your lawyer."

"I don't need my lawyer, Cord. No matter how much I wanted to wring the guy's neck, I did not kill Vincent Hamm."

"I know you didn't. Aside from the fact you're not that kind of guy, weren't you away around that time?"

Jesse made a sound of assent. "I've got nothing to hide, and the sooner your girlfriend realizes that, the better."

"Like I said, she's not my girlfriend."

Jesse chuckled. "But there's something going on, isn't there?"

The man was too damn astute. Yeah, there was something, but even he couldn't define the way Zoe Warren had crawled under his skin.

"She's a cop. Trust me, there's nothing going on," Cord said firmly.

"If you say so."

Their conversation drifted to ranching matters, and they eventually finished their call. Cord pocketed his phone and felt tension coil within his body. He wanted nothing more right now than to take his horse to the open pastures and go for a blistering ride. Anything to expend this pent-up energy that resided in a red-hot knot in the center of his gut.

He still couldn't believe the nerve of Detective Warren. The idea that the woman he'd left trembling last night had calmly gotten up this morning and gone straight to the hospital made him so mad he needed to do something to work it off. Preferably something to do with her. The random thought struck him square in the solar plexus, robbing him of breath. He strode through the house and out to the stables, the ride he'd been thinking of at the forefront of his mind. But then halfway through saddling up his favorite gelding, he hesitated and pulled his cell phone from his pocket.

Since he'd left Zoe Warren last night, he'd all but talked himself into staying away from her, but it seemed that would have to take a back seat. He needed to talk to the woman and set her straight about a few things. Clearly she hadn't been listening yesterday. He needed to ensure she listened to him today.

Zoe spent much of the middle part of the day back in her motel room working on her computer and going over all the information she had to date. No matter which way she looked at things, the answers she sought remained very firmly out of reach. She put in a call to her boss and apprised him of where she was so far. His response had not been heartening. Zoe's stomach grumbled, bemoaning the fact she hadn't picked up anything for lunch, when her reminder pinged to say it was time to meet the sheriff at the diner.

Her mouth watered the minute she set foot in the place. A wave from a booth near the front windows drew her attention, and she walked over to the sheriff and stuck out her hand.

"Sheriff Battle, good to see you again."

The sheriff stood and took her hand. "Call me Nate."

His grip was firm and dry, and unlike a lot of men she met in the line of duty, he didn't seem to feel the need to exert pressure and dominance over her by crushing the bones in her hands with the introductory gesture.

"Something sure smells good here," Zoe commented as she slid into the seat opposite him.

"I can recommend the pie. Of course, I am biased. This is my wife's business." He patted his firm stomach. "Hell of a job staying fit with that temptation in my life."

Zoe laughed. A waitress came over and poured her a coffee. She smiled her thanks and ordered a slice of pie to go with it. So what if it wasn't exactly healthy to eat pie for lunch this late in the day? A woman deserved a treat every now and then, right?

When the pie was delivered, she quickly sampled a bite and closed her eyes and made a blissful sound deep in her throat.

"Told you it was good," the sheriff said laconically as he leaned back against the red faux-leather booth.

"You weren't lying," Zoe agreed, quickly scooping up

another bite before putting her fork down and dabbing at her mouth with a paper napkin. It was time she got to the point. "What can you tell me about Jesse Stevens?"

"Jesse?" Nate Battle looked puzzled for all of two seconds. "I thought you were after Sterling Perry?"

"He's been cleared. So, Stevens?"

"You think he's got something to do with Vincent's murder?"

His tone was cautious, as if he was sounding her out, even though he clearly didn't believe she was on the right track. She explained about the voice mail message Stevens had left, then played the sound file from her phone.

"He sure sounds annoyed," the sheriff said mildly. "But that doesn't mean he did anything."

"You don't think he's capable of murder?" Zoe challenged.

"I didn't say that."

"But?" She knew he was leaving more unsaid.

"I just can't see it. The man's a hard worker, keeps to himself when necessary, steps up for the community through the Texas Cattleman's Club on a regular basis. But murder? No. Jesse's not the kind of guy to hold a grudge."

"Well, we'll see about that when I interview him."

Between her and the sheriff they arranged a suitable day and time. She wasn't worried that Jesse would run out of town. His devotion to his sister had been more than clear. He wouldn't be leaving her while she was in the hospital, and judging by how frail the young woman was, she'd probably need some continued care at home, too. There was no way Jesse was leaving anytime soon.

Thinking about Jesse led her thoughts to his neighbor. The guy had been defensive on his friend's behalf yesterday—and very distracting last night every time she'd tried to draw the conversation toward her investigation. Thinking about it this morning, once her mind had cleared from the unaccustomed haze of sensual fog he'd wrapped her in, she'd begun to wonder if his attention to her wasn't part of some greater scheme to distract her from her purpose.

"What do you know about Cord Galicia?" she blurted.

Battle gave her a strange look. Maybe because the instant she'd asked the question she felt heat begin to rise from her chest and up her throat. If she wasn't mistaken, she'd be breaking out in the nervous blotches of color that used to be her curse when she was a teenager facing a stressful situation.

"Cord? Well, he's Jesse's neighbor. They grew up together. Help one another out when necessary. They even learned to fly together back when they were in their late teens."

"But what about the man himself?"

The waitress came and poured the sheriff another coffee, and he took his time doctoring it how he liked it before he responded.

"He's a decent guy. You don't think he did it, do you? He and Jesse are tight, but Cord wouldn't commit murder for him."

"I don't know. Galicia was very protective of Stevens when I questioned him yesterday."

"You questioned him yesterday?" He blew out a breath. "You sure didn't waste any time upsetting the locals, did you? I thought we'd agreed to talk before you started questioning people."

She heard the note of censure in his voice. "I just wanted to get a feel for where people were situated on this thing. You can appreciate that my goal is to find whoever is guilty of Hamm's murder and charge them accordingly. I'm not here on vacation."

"I get that, but don't go off like a steer at a gate. Upset

folks and they'll close ranks and you'll get nothing out of them."

Zoe closed her eyes and breathed in deeply before opening them again. "I'm just doing my job. I've been living and breathing this case for months now. I want it solved."

"If it can be solved."

She didn't want to admit it, but he was right. "Yeah, there's that, too. The longer this takes, the harder it's going to be to find the evidence we need. Everything was compromised in the flood."

The sheriff's phone buzzed on the table in front of him and he glanced at the screen.

"I'm sorry, I'm going to have to take that."

"Go ahead."

She watched as he answered the call and got up to pace the sidewalk outside the diner. After a few minutes he shoved the phone into his pocket and came back inside.

"I have to go. Get in touch with my office to arrange a time to use the interview room. They'll make sure you have all the equipment you need."

"Thanks, Sheriff. I appreciate it."

"And call me before you go questioning my people, okay? You may actually get a better result if I come along with you."

"Noted, thanks."

She finished her pie and lingered over another coffee before heading to the sheriff's department, where she arranged to interview Jesse using their equipment. Apparently it would take a day or two to set up, because their camera and recording equipment were glitchy. While the news was frustrating, there was nothing she could do about it other than wait. There were probably worse places to cool her heels for a few days. The problem was she couldn't think of any right now.

* * *

Cord felt a whole ton better after a hard ride, but the irritation he'd felt over Zoe confronting Jesse at the hospital still prickled under his skin. He grabbed his phone and scrolled through his saved numbers, then punched the one he was looking for with a determined index finger. It rang three times before going to voice mail. Ha, she was avoiding him, was she? He contemplated hanging up without leaving a message, but where was the fun in that? Instead, he forced himself to smile as he spoke.

"I couldn't sleep last night for thinking about you. Call me."

Hopefully his message would rile her enough for her to call him. If not, well, he'd be paying her a visit. He was contemplating adding a hard swim in his pool to the ride he'd just had, when his phone buzzed in his pocket. A quick glance at the display brought a smile curling around his lips.

"Missing me?" he answered.

"Not at all," Zoe said breezily. "Did you want me for something?"

He hesitated, letting the silence play between them before speaking. "Now there's a leading question."

"Quit fooling, Galicia. Why did you call?"

"Come to the ranch for barbecued ribs tonight. Seven o'clock."

"What if I'm busy?"

"You gotta eat."

He could feel her indecision over the phone and chose his next words very carefully. "What are you afraid of, Zoe?"

"Not you," she answered swiftly.

He chuckled. "See you at seven."

He severed the call before she could respond. A smile

wreathed his face as he imagined her irritation at not having had the last word. It was kind of fun to keep her off-kilter just that little bit. To get where she was in her line of work, she had to be some kind of dogged control freak—turning over metaphorical stones and looking for clues every day. He'd bet she wasn't used to someone making decisions for her, and he really liked that, in this instance, it was him doing it.

She'd turn up tonight—he'd bet his newly weaned calves on it.

The entire drive to the Galicia spread, Zoe cursed under her breath. The arrogance of the man, ordering her around like that. *But you're going there, aren't you?* a voice in the back of her mind taunted. *You want to see him again.*

"Shut up!" she said aloud.

Or maybe you just want him?

The question rattled around in her mind as she rolled through the gates and up the long driveway to his house. He'd gotten her off so damn fast last night that he'd left her reeling. She hadn't even known she could feel so much so quickly. For her, lovemaking had always been a long, slow buildup, not always followed by release. But with him? It had been mere minutes. And every sensation he'd wrought from her had made her want more.

So, yeah, she was prepared to admit she wanted him. She couldn't continue to fool herself that she was coming out here to question him about Jesse Stevens, especially when Stevens himself had said he'd turn up for the recorded interview in a couple of days.

Zoe stopped her car and got out, staring at the house for the second time in as many days and admiring the stone exterior. The place looked solid, durable and reliable. *A reflection of its master?* she wondered. There was movement at the door, and Cord Galicia strode out, his presence commanding her eye from the second he came through the doorway.

Yes, *master* was the right term for him. Master of all he surveyed? *He might like to think so.* She smiled inwardly. But he was no master to her. She'd come here because she wanted to, not because he'd all but ordered her presence.

"I'm glad you came," he said as she approached the front entrance.

"Ribs are my weakness," she answered with as much insouciance as she could muster.

He showed her inside and then led her through the house and outside to a loggia. The scent of hickory smoke hung in the air and, combined with the aroma of barbecuing meat, made Zoe's mouth water in anticipation.

"What can I get you to drink? Wine?"

"No wine for me, not when I have to drive back to town," Zoe protested.

"You could always stay."

Her inner muscles tightened on a swell of desire at the simplicity of his words. She shouldn't have been surprised. She'd been half expecting it, hadn't she? Half *wanting* it, too?

"We'll see," she answered, keeping her words deliberately evasive.

"Wine it is, then."

She didn't argue when he poured two glasses of red wine and passed one to her.

"Thanks. The ribs smell good."

"They are good."

"Oh, you're so confident of your ability?"

"Abuelita's secret recipe," he said with a sly wink.

"Not so secret if you know it," Zoe felt compelled to point out.

"True, but she spent a lot of time showing me how to look after myself. She also told me that to win the heart of a good woman, a man needs to know how to do more than reheat a can of beans."

Zoe laughed. "Is that what you're doing? Trying to win my heart?"

As soon as she said the words, she realized they'd have been better left unsaid. A shadow passed over Cord's face and his light mood changed.

"Just offering some Royal hospitality while you're here," he said before taking a sip of wine. "What do you think of the wine?"

She took a sip, too. "Mmm, it's good, like velvet. I like how it doesn't leave a dry aftertaste on your tongue."

"It'll taste even better with the ribs."

He gestured for her to take a seat on the large outdoor rattan sofa, and she sank comfortably against the overstuffed pillows. He lowered himself in the seat opposite.

"A girl could fall asleep here if she wasn't careful," she commented.

"Didn't sleep so good last night?"

A flush stained her cheeks. "Look, about last night."

"Hmm?"

He looked at her over the rim of his glass, and at the heat in his gaze Zoe felt her toes curl in her sensible low-heeled shoes.

She shook her head. "Never mind. Least said, soonest mended."

He laughed. "Is that something your grandmother used to say?"

She smiled a little. "Yeah."

"Zoe," he said as he leaned forward, his gaze intense. "Last night was merely an appetizer."

Six

Cord wasn't sure what devil of impulse had driven him to say that to her, but it was satisfying to watch the play of raw emotion that danced across her features. He could pinpoint the exact moment she decided to take control.

"Is that so?" she asked, arching a dark brow at him. "We'll see about that."

"Yes." He nodded. "We will."

Again he had the satisfaction of seeing her lose her tenuous grip on the conversation, and he decided to turn things to more general matters. He didn't want to alienate her entirely. It was enough, for now, that she was here.

"What do you do in your spare time?" he asked, reaching for the bottle and topping off her glass.

"Spare time?" She laughed. "What's that?"

"You're a workaholic?"

"Aren't you? You can't run a spread as big as this one without long hours, right?"

He tipped his head in acknowledgment. "But I have people I delegate to. An experienced foreman, ranch hands. Are you telling me your work is your life?"

"My work is a very important part of my life. I want to be the best."

"Better than your dad."

"Better than everyone in my family."

He looked at her a little closer. Being the youngest in a testosterone-heavy family had obviously left its scars. Zoe Warren felt she had something to prove to the males in her family, and it had to be proven on their battleground.

"What would you have done if you hadn't been a cop?"

"I never wanted to be anything else, much to my mom's great disappointment. After four boys she thought she could raise a kindred spirit. Someone who might enjoy shopping with her, attending high teas or getting pampered at the beauty shop. But that's not me. It doesn't mean she's given up on me, though," Zoe finished saying with a deep chuckle.

"Sounds like an intrepid woman."

"She is. I admire her, a lot. It can't be easy to see every person you love step out the door every day and have to wonder whether or not they'll come home safely."

Cord felt that unwelcome clench around his heart that he always got when reminded of Britney. He knew exactly what Zoe was talking about, and he knew just how much it hurt when that loved one didn't come home again. He put his glass onto the wooden table between them and got up to check on the ribs, anything to put a little distance between him and the reminder that while he may be powerfully attracted to Zoe Warren, she was first, last and always a police officer. He wouldn't go through that again.

The ribs were almost done. His grandmother would have been proud.

"I'm just going to grab the salad and corn bread. Be back in a minute," he said in Zoe's direction.

"Can I help?"

"Nope. You just stay right there," he said firmly.

As large as his kitchen was, he didn't want to be moving around it with her behind him. After last night he was struggling to keep his hands and his mouth to himself, and it had taken some effort to play the considerate host. To pass her a glass of wine without touching her fingers. To watch her sample the beverage without leaning forward to kiss the residue from her lips.

Damn, he was getting hard just thinking about it. To distract himself he went to the large double fridge and pulled out the bowl of salad he'd prepared shortly before her arrival. Setting it on a tray, he then grabbed the basket of corn bread he'd put in the oven to warm. He already had utensils and plates in an old painted wooden sideboard out in the loggia.

"You look very domesticated," Zoe commented as he quickly set the outdoor table and lit a bunch of squat candles in the center of the table.

"I'm a man of many talents. Come, take a seat," he suggested. "I'll get the ribs off the grill."

He plated up the ribs and brought the platter to the table.

"You mentioned your grandmother. Did she raise you?" Zoe asked as he settled into his place.

"Both my grandparents were still here with us when my father took over the ranch. My grandfather died five years ago but Abuelita is still fighting fit. She lives with my parents. When Dad retired, he decided he wanted to get away from ranching. Told me that if he lived here, or near here, he'd always be interfering in my way of doing things and he didn't think that was fair. They bought a condo in Palm Springs, but to be honest, I don't think he's happy there. Oh, he puts on a good face and all, but he's a farm boy at heart. Rounds of golf and cocktails at five?" Cord shook his head. "That's not his lifestyle."

"I guess he made his choice, though, right?"

"It worries me that he's unhappy. His pride won't let him admit he's made a mistake. I would welcome him back. His knowledge is invaluable, and God knows the house is big enough for us all to continue living here without tripping over one another. It worked for him and his parents. I don't see why it wouldn't have worked for us." He shrugged. "Whatever, it is what it is."

"I couldn't wait to move out of home and get a place of my own. Even though my brothers are all married, I just felt suffocated by my family's expectations of me."

"Their expectations?" Cord probed.

"I'm a girl. They want me to settle down and have babies."

"And quit your career?"

Her laugh was scornful. "They don't see this as my career. It's a placeholder to them, until I do the right thing and find a good man and settle down and let him support me. My family is fiercely traditional."

"Well, there's traditional and there's dark ages," Cord commiserated.

He picked up the wine bottle and held it above her glass without pouring, just waiting for her assent or refusal. There was no way she'd be legal to drive if she had another glass of wine. They both knew it. If she accepted the drink, she was staying. It wasn't until he allowed the thought to form again in his mind that he realized just how much he wanted her to stay. How much he wanted to explore her again. The moment Zoe's fingers lightly grasped the slender stem of the wineglass and lifted it toward the bottle, every particle in his body stirred.

Her blue eyes met his and locked. He saw the faint remnants of indecision fade and be replaced by something else. Heat. Need. Desire. He slowly tipped the bottle and poured.

"Thank you," she said, lifting the glass to her lips and taking a sip.

"No, thank you," Cord said, his voice no more than a rumble.

He dragged his focus back to their meal, to the succulent meat that, with a gentle bite, simply twisted off the ribs, then melted on the tongue in a burst of flavors. But right now his taste buds were flooded with the memory of Zoe's skin from last night, and the longing to repeat the experience—and more.

He couldn't say how he got through the rest of the meal or what they discussed. All he could think about was the fact that Zoe Warren was staying the night. Sure, she might yet take him up on the guest-room idea, but he had a feeling that she'd be sleeping with him. Actually, sleeping was the furthest thing from his mind. The anticipation of how the rest of their night would unfold settled around him, filling him with a sizzling buzz of excitement. Yeah, this was going to be a good night. He would put aside the reasons she'd come here and what she did for a living, and he'd make damn sure she forgot them, too.

Zoe felt herself relax in increments. It had to be the wine she'd unwisely drunk, she told herself. It would have nothing to do with the man sitting opposite her. The man who'd put together a meal that was worthy of any five-star restaurant, because even in its simplicity, it had been imbued with a myriad of flavors that varied in intensity but each of which created both craving and satisfaction. A bit like the man himself.

And just like that she didn't feel quite so relaxed anymore. She'd made a conscious decision here tonight. The moment she'd accepted his offer of wine, she knew she'd be staying—and forget about any guest room. The hum of her body had heightened to a persistent buzz of need, and the idea of taking care of that need on her own held little appeal when there was a warm and willing partner right here in front of her. She allowed herself to revel in the air of expectancy that built between herself and Cord Galicia.

When they finished their food, Cord began to clear their things away. Zoe swiftly rose to assist him.

"You don't need to help. You're my guest here tonight," Cord protested.

"Of course I'm helping you," she answered firmly, stacking plates and cutlery.

She followed him through to the kitchen, where she rinsed dishes while he stacked the state-of-the-art dishwasher. Clearly ranching was a profitable business for this family, not that money impressed her necessarily, but she liked seeing people enjoy the fruits of their hard labor—even if it was something as simple as a dishwasher. She made a passing comment, complimenting Cord on his choice in kitchenware. He laughed.

"You think I had anything to do with any of this?" He flung out his arms to encapsulate the entire room. "No way. When Dad declared his retirement, my mom and Abuelita took it as a chance to ensure that I didn't have to lift more than a finger without a woman here to look after me. Everything was changed. You just about need a software degree to operate the oven, let alone the microwave."

Zoe laughed along with him, but inside she felt something pull tight and close up like a clamshell. Clearly there

was an expectation in this family that the women took
care of their men. Not that looking after a household and
all the multiple things that fell under that umbrella was in
any way less important than what she did, but to Zoe her
career was everything. She wouldn't give it up for anyone.

And no one is asking you to, that voice in the back of her
mind reminded her tersely. *Basically you're here to satisfy
an urge. Don't expect any more than that, nor any less.*

With that voice ringing clearly in her mind, Zoe cocked
her head and watched Cord as he completed the cleanup.
There was something very satisfying about watching a
strong and capable man busy in the pursuit of domestic duties. Sexy even. Yeah, definitely sexy. Cord had big, strong
hands with long, deft fingers. He kept his nails short and
clean, but there was no denying those hands had calluses
earned through hard work and determination. And yet they
could be gentle, too, she thought on a shiver of memory.

"Everything okay?" Cord said as he turned to face her.

"Oh yes," she replied. "Just thinking about dessert."

"Dessert?"

"Yeah. You said last night was the appetizer. You've just
fed me dinner. Which kind of leaves…" She let her voice
trail away suggestively.

"Dessert."

He took a step closer, and Zoe felt the heat in the room
skip up a few notches. When he reached out a hand to
stroke her face with his fingertips, it was all she could
do not to throw herself into his arms. Instead, she stood
there, her eyes locked with his, her body all but visibly
shaking as she waited to see what he would do next. She
didn't have to wait long.

Cord moved fast, his arms going around her and one
hand cupping the back of her head as he lowered his face
to hers and took her lips in a searing kiss that all but turned

her legs to water. Hot, steaming water, but boneless none-theless. She reveled in the feel of his firm body as he hauled her against him, plastering her soft curves against his harder frame. And she lost herself in the taste of him—hot, sinful, spicy and sweet all at once.

Suddenly he was moving away from her, his hand clasping one of hers firmly as he tugged her after him.

"We're not doing this here," he said in a gravelly tone.

"As impressed as I am by your appliances, I concur with your decision," she teased in return.

He threw her a grin over his shoulder and headed for the staircase. She followed close behind as he continued down a carpeted hallway to the end, where he threw open a door and yanked her inside.

"I want you naked," he said in a voice that brooked no argument.

"How convenient. I want the same of you," she said bluntly and began to peel her clothing from her body.

Opposite her, Cord undressed just as quickly. She could barely keep her eyes off him. The sinewy strength of his arms showed in the way his muscles bunched and released as he dragged off his shirt with little respect for the buttons that tore free and bounced onto the carpet beneath their feet. He kicked off his boots and shucked his jeans and socks in a smooth movement, which left him standing there in front of her in only his boxer briefs. Clad in only her bra and panties, red lace this time, she eyed his very obvious erection constrained behind the cotton knit of his briefs. She sucked in her bottom lip and bit down hard to hold back the moan of delight that threatened to break free.

Cord, too, was taking a moment to feast his eyes on her body.

"Red lace? Ah, Detective, you slay me," he groaned as he moved forward to take her into his arms.

The shock of their skin touching made her draw in a sharp breath, which in turn made her breasts swell. The heat of his chest poured through her lacy bra, and she wished she'd been faster to disrobe so she could feel him more closely, without any barriers between them. She shifted, reaching her arms behind her only to feel him trap them in his hands.

"Not so fast, Detective. I think I want to enjoy the sight of you just a little longer."

He carefully walked her backward until she felt the softness of bed linen behind her knees.

"On the bed," he ordered.

"Are you always this bossy in the bedroom?" she asked.

But even as she said the words, she did as he'd commanded because she was eager to feel him against her again. Eager to feel him everywhere.

"Well, we'd have to do this more than once for you to have a basis for comparison, wouldn't we?" he responded.

She laughed. "Bossy and confident. What a combination."

"You forgot something else," he said as he hooked his thumbs into the waistband of his briefs. "I'm also very, very good at what I do."

Her mouth dried and her voice was little more than a croak when she spoke. "Ah yes, I'd forgotten. Perhaps you could refresh my memory."

His smile was feral and made every cell in her body clench on a wave of anticipation. Had she provoked the beast? It would seem so. He slid his briefs off his hips, freeing his straining erection to her hungry gaze.

"Mmm, dessert," she managed before he moved onto the bed.

"I'm not sure if you've earned your dessert yet," he murmured against her ear.

"Oh? Tell me what I've done wrong."

"Well, let's see. There's the matter of you pestering Jesse and his sister today."

"Not to have done so would be in dereliction of my duty."

"I'd asked you not to," he said, taking an earlobe between his teeth and biting gently.

Zoe squirmed as sensation shot through her.

"Actually," she said, breathless now, "you ordered me not to."

"You admit you were disobedient?"

He nipped a trail down her neck, while one hand brushed against her bra, rasping against her budded nipple before his fingers closed around the aching peak and squeezed just right. It felt like he already knew every intimate secret about her erogenous zones because he managed to zero in immediately on every one.

"I admit nothing," she gasped as he squeezed her nipple more firmly. "Besides, I have to wait until the sheriff's office equipment is repaired before I can interview him properly."

A spear of pleasure shot straight to the apex of her thighs and she squirmed again. She could feel her panties getting wet as her need for him increased in rapidly expanding increments.

"Equipment?" he asked, nuzzling against her skin, his hot breath making her feel even hotter.

"Yeah, video camera and recording equipment. Have to do things by the letter. But why are we talking about this? Haven't you got something more important to attend to?"

"More important?" He lifted his head and looked at her with a teasing glow in his eyes.

"Yeah—me."

He laughed. "Bossy, Detective. I see I'm going to have

to continue my investigation a little more carefully, just to remind you who's in charge here," he promised, his voice deadly serious.

His wet, hot mouth replaced his fingers at her breast.

"Cord, please," she begged, without even knowing exactly what she was begging for.

"Please—now that sounds nice. Please what? Please bite you?"

She groaned but nodded her assent.

"Your wish is my command," he said, his voice getting rougher with each touch he bestowed on her.

She felt his erection against her as he lowered himself and bit her gently through her bra.

"Naked, please. I want to be naked. This isn't fair."

"Fair? The detective wants fair?"

She felt his fingers at the clasp of her bra, felt her breasts spill free as the fabric mercifully fell away. Then there was nothing but sensation as he kissed and licked her heated flesh. She arched beneath him, desperate for her skin to meet with his, desperate for his touch lower down her body, where she ached with a hunger that was all consuming.

"Don't rush, Zoe. Some delights are best savored slowly," he teased as he spent more time first on one tautly beaded nipple and then the other. "Ah, you taste divine. I could do this all night long."

"Surely not all night… I may melt apart in your arms before that."

"Well, maybe not all night, then," he conceded with a chuckle. "Are you always so pedantic?"

"Details are my thing," she admitted on a rushed breath as he began to trail that wicked mouth of his down the center of her rib cage and lower to her belly button.

"I'm finding I like pretty much everything there is about you, Detective," Cord drawled.

"I have to admit I'm enjoying your journey of discovery."

He laughed again, and Zoe thrilled on the sound of it. Sex had been infrequent but good, but even so, she'd never enjoyed this level of fun in the process. Nor this level of aching demand that throbbed through her. If he kept this up, he'd have only to breathe on her clit and she'd be transported to the stratosphere. She could feel her body pulse as Cord continued his voyage lower, and lower still—but not quite low enough or fast enough for her satisfaction.

"I like what you've done here," he said, pulling back a little and stroking her neatly groomed body hair. "Intriguing. Hard to maintain?"

"Seriously, you're asking me about my personal grooming?"

"Why not? It hasn't distracted me from your punishment."

He pressed a kiss on her mound. Close, but still too far from her aching bud for her liking.

"Laser hair removal, and a regular trim." She ground out the words.

He kissed her again, a tiny bit closer to her clit, to her release. She shivered and pressed her head back into the pillow as he traced his fingertips up the inside of her thigh. Shivers rippled through her.

"Consider me punished," she begged. "Just please, touch me."

"Like this?" he asked, slowly pressing one finger into her wet core.

He stroked her, dragging a sound from her that spoke volumes to her level of need.

"More."

"And still the lady thinks she's in control." He sighed and withdrew his finger.

At her moan of distress he pressed two fingers inside

her and stroked her again, and then, at last, he closed his mouth around the aching, pulsing bead of flesh that had been his goal all along.

"Mmm, dessert," Cord said against her heated skin.

Zoe began to laugh, but then he changed the pressure of his tongue, moved his fingers, and all humor was suspended as he sent her soaring on a pounding wave of pleasure so intense she lost all sense of who and where she was. All she knew was the man who had delivered this pleasure was virtually a stranger to her, and right now she didn't care.

It was some time later before Zoe felt herself come back to any kind of awareness. Cord was lying on his side next to her, one arm bent under his head, his free hand softly stroking her belly.

"You're not going to leave me now, are you?" she asked, lifting a hand to trace the strong lines of his face.

"Nope," he said simply. "Not this time. Besides, we're at my place and I'm not letting you go anywhere."

"Good," she replied. "Because I want you inside me."

"Making demands of me now?"

"Yeah, got a problem with that?"

He flashed her a smile. "Not at all."

"But first…"

"First?"

"*My* dessert."

Zoe moved quickly to sit astride him. Beneath her bottom she could feel his erection, but that would have to wait awhile. First, she wanted to bestow on him a little of the same punishment he'd dealt to her. Cord's hands moved to grasp her hips but she shook her head.

"Uh-uh," she cautioned. "No touching. Not yet. Hold on to the headboard until I say you can move."

"Are you planning to frisk me, Detective?"

"I've told you, I'm conducting an investigation," she said with a playful curl of her lips. "A very important investigation."

She trailed her fingertips along the underside of his upper arms. His skin was softer there—deliciously so. As she traced around his armpits to the top of his rib cage, she felt his skin grow goose bumps at her touch.

"Do you like that?" she whispered.

"Oh yeah."

He shifted a little beneath her, and she lifted one finger to caution him.

"Don't make me get my cuffs."

"You brought cuffs to dinner?"

"And my gun. They're in my handbag along with my badge. I never leave home without them."

"Duly noted," Cord said with a slight frown.

Zoe hesitated in her movements, leaning back a little to study his face. His eyes still glittered with desire but his expression had become more closed, less playful.

"Does it worry you I carry a gun everywhere?"

She began to stroke his smooth chest, her fingertips tingling at the sensation of her skin on his.

"Not my place to worry about you."

"That's right, it's not. Enough talking. Now, just feel."

And she made sure he did. She smoothed her hands flat and skimmed the muscles of his chest, learning the dips and curves that made up the appealing shapes of his body, from his broad shoulders to his narrow waist. She bent down and kissed him before transferring her mouth from his lips to the flat discs of his nipples. They drew into small peaks against her tongue as she pinched and played with him. His hips shifted again and she clamped her thighs tight around him, halting his movement. Let him suffer the way he'd made her suffer—although it had been a delectable torment that he'd made her endure before bringing her to completion, and she had every intention of ensuring he experienced the same level of satisfaction.

And if he didn't? Well, she'd have to go back to square one and start over again. Her mouth curved into another smile at the thought, and she applied her attention to making him squirm beneath her as she tasted, licked and sucked at his skin. He wore a subtle cologne, but it was his own special scent that she'd quickly become addicted to. It made her want to nuzzle against him and draw in deep breath after deep breath. Never before had she felt this visceral level of attraction to another person, and it was intoxicating.

She rose up slightly and shifted her legs lower as she explored his torso, delighting in the way his skin jumped beneath her tongue as she followed the light trail of hair from his belly button down to his groin. His erection left her in no doubt as to his readiness, but she wanted to prolong this as much as possible. She let her tongue drift along the shadowed line of his inner hip—down, then up again. The hitch in his breathing told her that she was tormenting him, but to his credit he kept his hands firmly attached to the headboard, even though the muscles of his arms were bunched with tension.

Maybe it was time to take pity on him, she thought, and she turned her attention to his swollen shaft. She nuzzled at the base, breathing in the hot, musky scent of his skin, then trailed her tongue from base to tip. Cord groaned out loud at her actions, his hands suddenly letting go of the headboard and coming to cup her head, his fingers tangling in her short hair. She licked him again before taking the hot, silky head into her mouth and playing her tongue against the smoothness. His fingers tightened, and she felt his entire body clench as he fought against the urge to thrust deeper into her mouth.

Suddenly it became important to her to make him lose control, and she used every trick she'd ever read about as she licked, sucked and stroked him to a wild, shaking climax. When he was spent, she shifted until she was lying beside him, her head nestled against his chest, her arm across his waist. His heart beat like a herd of stampeding cattle in his chest and his body glistened with a light sheen of perspiration.

She'd done that to him, she thought with a touch of pride. She'd reduced this man—who had at first appeared to be fierce and determined, but who could cook like a dream, who could bring her to orgasm with a deftness she'd never known before—to one who'd put all sense of responsibility and control aside to revel in pure gratification. It was empowering to know she'd done that for him, liberating to realize that she could meet him on an even playing field where there were no specific roles based on gender. Only sensation, and pleasure and, she smiled anew, fun. Her time in Royal was shaping up to be very interesting indeed.

Seven

Cord waited some time until he could trust himself to speak again.

"That wasn't how I envisaged this evening happening," he stated bluntly.

Zoe continued tracing tiny shapes with her fingertips at his waist.

"Oh, disappointed?" she teased.

He felt something swell in his chest. Happiness? It had been so long since he'd felt anything like it, let alone trusted anyone with his body the way he'd trusted Zoe, that he found it hard to define.

"Definitely not disappointed," he growled. Cord rolled over so Zoe lay beneath him, his face directly over hers. "But I feel like we could do better."

She laughed—a deep-seated chuckle that made her whole body shake.

"By all means let's try it. You can never have too much dessert, after all."

She was a woman after his own heart, it seemed, and this time, when they made love, he made certain that, despite several delightful detours, they joined as one, thanking his lucky stars that the condoms in his drawer hadn't expired. He knew, because he'd checked before she arrived tonight, and while he hadn't wanted to assume this night would end with them both in his bed, he was so very glad it had.

Her long, supple legs hooked around his waist when he entered her, her heat and inner muscles drawing him in deep. Cord locked his gaze with hers, watched as her eyes became glassy as they rocked together in a dance as old as time. He felt her entire body clench on the first wave of orgasm as it hit her, and he allowed himself free rein, until they reached the summit together and hung there suspended in mutual bliss, before descending back to reality.

Morning came all too soon. In the distance, Cord could hear the sounds of his hands out on the ranch moving cattle, the lowing beasts voicing their thoughts on being brought in to a new pasture. He should be out there, working alongside them, but a certain tall, dark-haired detective was still entangled in his sheets. Not that he was complaining. She felt good—too good. Too easy to get used to and that sure wouldn't be a good thing. Not only did she live in Houston, she was a cop. A dedicated one at that. She wasn't in her career for a few years to pass time. No, this was a lifetime choice for her.

He hadn't been intimate with anyone since Britney, which probably explained why this thing with Zoe had flared up so quickly. There was no way it could be long-term. Fires that burned this brightly extinguished just as swiftly.

He thought about her bag downstairs, about the gun

she'd admitted was secreted in there. Even on a social visit, she was armed. It was part and parcel of who she was, and the danger that was associated with the kind of people she tracked down was equally a part of her every day.

He'd thought he could handle it with Britney. He'd supported her in her dream to become a cop, told her he'd be there for her 100 percent. But his support didn't equate to squat when she faced down a liquor-store robber only a few hours into her first shift. And being there as they pulled life support in ICU days after she'd been shot—well, that had been unarguably the darkest day of his life. He would not go down that road again. He simply could not.

Rebuilding himself had been hard, but his parents had put off their planned early retirement to see him back on his feet. His *abuelita* had been a strong, silent presence at his back, feeding his body and feeding his soul whenever he would let her. He'd resumed a life, of sorts. He'd dated once or twice, but things had never gotten to the stage they had with Zoe. Hell, he didn't even understand how things had moved this fast with her.

She was everything he never again wanted in a woman. Career focused, a detective and undoubtedly fiercely independent. She'd have had to fight her way into her position—past the expectations of her family that she fit into a more traditional mold, and past the obstacles that she no doubt had to overcome to be recognized in her working world. He'd always told himself that if he ever took the risk of another relationship again, it would be with a woman without career-focused ambition. One who shared the same dreams and goals as he had and who would partner with him in everything to do with life on the ranch. One who wanted stability, security and who had a desire to continue to build a legacy for future generations of Galicia children.

There was a sharp stab in his chest at the thought of

kids. He'd always taken for granted that he'd be a father one day, but now he wasn't so sure. That took a level of commitment he wasn't certain he was capable of anymore—not only to the children themselves, but to their mother, too. One thing was for certain, though—a woman like Zoe Warren was not on the same life path as he was. The whole city-versus-country thing would never work between them. He loved life on the ranch. He'd been born and bred into it as much as she'd been born and bred into her life in Houston. They were chalk and cheese, oil and water—and yet he couldn't seem to get enough of her.

Zoe stirred and stretched, untangling her limbs from his and rolling onto her back. Cord let his gaze slide over the lean lines of her body and then back to the surprising fullness of her breasts. Now that he knew how sensitive they were, he dreamed of ways he could tease them into the taut peaks that spoke evocatively of her depth of desire.

"Good morning," he said, his voice still a little gruff with sleep.

"How good is yet to be determined. On the meal basis we've covered appetizers, main courses and dessert. What's breakfast like around here?"

Never one to back down from a challenge, he showed her, and it was a full half hour later before he chased her into the bathroom, where they showered together. He would have taken her there again if he hadn't run out of condoms, but he had to satisfy himself with soaping her up and washing her hair and helping her rinse off. When she exited the shower stall, he switched the water to cold, determined to get his body under some semblance of control, but one look at her as she wiped her body dry with one of his thick, fluffy towels and he knew it was an exercise in hopelessness. The only way he'd return to any kind of normal was when she'd gone, and oddly, he didn't want her to leave.

She was dressed when he came into the bedroom with a towel wrapped firmly around his waist.

"I have to go," she said with obvious reluctance. "Thanks for dinner and…everything."

"Anytime," he drawled in response. "In fact, how about dinner tonight? We can go to the Texas Cattleman's Club."

"I've heard about it. Isn't the dress code pretty strict in the restaurant there?"

"I could lend you a suit," he offered only half tongue in cheek. In fact, the more he thought about her in one of his suits wearing that sinfully seductive lingerie underneath, the more he liked the idea.

"I'll sort something out. What time?"

"I'll pick you up at seven thirty."

"I'll be ready."

The second he heard her car start and head down the driveway, he grabbed his cell phone and dialed the number of an old school friend.

"Frank, you working on the sheriff's recording and video equipment?"

"Yeah, but how'd you know that?"

Cord's hand tightened on his phone. "That's not important. Tell me, how long do you think it'll take to get it all up and running again?"

Frank hemmed and hawed a little before speaking. "Should be done by the end of the day."

He started to get into some of the technical jargon that made Cord's eyes cross, so Cord interrupted him the moment Frank drew in a breath.

"Look, you remember how I bailed you out with Sissy when she thought you were having an affair. Gave you an alibi?"

"Yeah?" There was a note of caution in Frank's voice that hadn't been there before.

"You owe me one, right?"

"Sure do," Frank agreed.

Cord closed his eyes briefly. He hated having to do this. He knew Frank hadn't been unfaithful to his wife. Sissy had been feeling insecure when she was pregnant, and it was easier for Cord to say he'd been with Frank than for Frank's biggest secret—the fact that he was learning to read as an adult, so he could read to his newborn child—to come out to all and sundry.

"Could you take a little longer over that repair?" Cord eventually asked.

"Like a day or two more?"

"How about a week, maybe two?"

"And then we'd be even?"

"More than even."

"I could do that," Frank agreed.

"Thanks, Frank, appreciate it."

"You gonna tell me why you want me to delay on this?"

"No."

"Okay, then. Sounds like I'll be struggling to source a vital thingymabobwotsit."

"Darn hard things to track down," Cord agreed with a smile before ending the call.

Ryder Currin rode the elevator to Sterling Perry's floor determined to put this old rivalry to bed once and for all. The pain and damage it was causing had gone on long enough.

"Mr. Currin!" the receptionist gasped, recognizing him instantly as he swept out of the elevator and past the main reception area. "You can't—"

"Don't bother announcing me. I'll announce myself," he said over his shoulder as he strode toward Perry's office.

He heard the scuffle of activity behind him, but no one was going to stop him now. He'd had enough. The roll-on effect of Perry's bitterness, fed by years of lies and innuendo from everyone around them, had taken a toll far greater than either man could ever have anticipated. And, as far as Ryder was concerned, it stopped now. It was one thing for Perry to hold a grudge because of Ryder's close friendship with Perry's late wife, Tamara, but quite another for him to stand in the way of his daughter Angela's happiness. Ryder's relationship with Angela had been fragile from the get-go, but despite that they'd found a way to make it work—until the old rumors of Ryder's relationship with her mom had resurfaced. Ryder and Tamara Perry had never been more than friends back when he'd worked as a hand on the York ranch—close friends, sure, but nothing more than that. He'd been her shoulder to cry on when things got tough and when he'd questioned her happiness in her marriage to Sterling, she'd made it clear her loyalty to her husband was unswerving and she would always remain with him, no matter what.

In the face of the vicious claims that had begun to circulate Ryder knew there'd be a wedge driven between him and Angela or Angela and her father, and she'd have to choose between them. Out of respect for both Tamara's memory and for her daughter, who he loved more than life itself, he'd walked away from Angela and his promise to marry her because there was no way he was forcing her to make that choice. He'd regretted his actions every second of every day since. He couldn't work things out with Angela until he'd worked things out with Perry.

Perry's manipulation of those around him had done a lot of damage, but the older man's meddling had resulted in an unexpected bonus and thanking him would be Ryder's starting point. Thanks to Perry's anonymous labor complaint—one that unfortunately had a strong basis in fact and that Ryder had known nothing about until the complaint had been brought to his attention—he'd been able to institute worker reforms. Firing Willem Inwood had been unpleasant, but regrettably necessary. No one got away with treating his staff badly, especially not someone in a position of privilege and respect such as Inwood had held.

Just the thought of the man was enough to get Ryder's dander up, and he forced himself to shove his anger down deep before it could potentially damage the impromptu meeting he was about to have with Sterling Perry. Like he always told his kids—Xander, Annabel and Maya—never approach anything or anyone important in anger. He stopped in his tracks, squared his shoulders and took a steadying breath. At his destination, Ryder knocked twice, then pushed open the door to Perry's office. The older man was just putting down his phone.

"You'd better be quick," Sterling said with a sardonic curl of his lip. "I'm informed security is on their way."

"Tell them to stand down. I'm not here to fight with you."

"Really? Forgive me if I don't believe you," he taunted.

"Well, you can believe it. In fact, I'm here to thank you."

"Oh?" Perry's brows rose in genuine surprise.

"Yeah. Thanks to your anonymous—" Ryder made air quotes with his fingers "—complaint, I was able to cut the rot from my business and institute reforms to ensure such abuses never happen again. We'll be stronger than ever now, and it's all thanks to you."

He watched the play of emotions across Perry's face. It wasn't often the man let his facade down, and it was enlightening to see the short burst of confusion followed by reluctant acceptance.

"I see," Perry replied, leaning back in his chair. "You'd better take a seat."

Ryder sat in the chair nearest to him, just as security arrived in the room.

"Mr. Perry, we'll deal with your unexpected visitor right away."

"No need. It appears that Mr. Currin and I have some business to discuss. Please leave us." Perry waved a hand toward the door.

"You want us to wait outside?"

"That won't be necessary, thank you."

Ryder waited until Perry's muscle left the room. Had he really wanted to hurt the older man, there was no way his security detail had been here quick enough. Ryder made a comment to that effect, eliciting a burst of unexpected laughter from the man who'd become his nemesis.

"You're giving me advice now? What's going on? Has the world turned upside down?" Perry commented with his signature brand of cynicism.

"Not upside down, not yet, anyway. But we need to talk. Settle things once and for all."

"I have nothing to settle with you. As far as I'm concerned, you're nothing more than a burr under my saddle. Now that you and Angela are no longer engaged, I can rest happy in the knowledge that, aside from today, I need never face you again."

Ryder let the man's words roll over him. The bitterness in the other man's tone was deep-seated and went back twenty-five long and often unhappy years. Ryder didn't want the next twenty-five to be the same. Somehow they had to reach a reconciliation of sorts. If they couldn't, he'd never be able to go back to Angela and beg her forgiveness

for walking away on their love, their life, their future together. That knowledge forced him to remain calm in the
face of Perry's veiled insults.

He drew in a deep breath. "Look, I know you hate my
guts—"

"That would require effort I wouldn't even bother ex-
pending," Sterling said as if the conversation bored him.

"You still resent my friendship with your late wife."

"Your relationship with Tamara was inappropriate,"
Sterling replied, biting back. "But she chose me. She always chose me."

"I know, but I want you to know that I never had an
affair with her. I'll swear it on a stack of Bibles if it will
help you to believe me, but as much as I admired and respected her, I never touched her. Not that way. We were
friends, that's all."

Sterling shook his head. "Why should I believe you?
You've not long come from my daughter's bed. What
kind of man are you, anyway? First the mother? Then my
daughter? That's just sick."

Disgust dripped from his every word.

"It would be sick if it were true. But I did not sleep
with Tamara, ever. And my relationship with Angela is
completely different. I loved Tamara, sure, as a friend, as
a mentor in many ways, and I certainly didn't think you
deserved her. Still don't, to be honest. But like you said,
she remained with you and she remained true to her vows
to you until her death, as well. For better or worse, Perry,
she loved you and only you."

There must have been something in his words that
started to sink in, because the hardened set to Perry's face
began to soften. Not a lot, but enough for Ryder to begin
to hope that maybe they could get past this at long last.

"So what if what you're telling me is the truth? It doesn't

change the things you've done since. The land you inherited from Tamara's father—the land that was so rich it oil it made your damn fortune—should always have been ours, not yours."

"You want it back in your family's hands?"

"Damn straight I do."

"Then give me your blessing to marry Angela."

The air between them crackled with barely restrained energy.

"Impossible. You broke off your engagement. She won't have you back."

"She will if she knows she doesn't have to choose between us. Angela loves me and I love her. We deserve to be happy. We deserve to be together."

"Why? You couldn't win her mother from me, so now you're settling for my daughter?"

"If I weren't a decent man I'd punch you in the mouth for that remark," Ryder growled through gritted teeth. "How dare you speak of your daughter so disparagingly. She deserves way better than that."

"I could argue that she deserves way better than you," Sterling spat back in return.

Ryder clenched his hands tight and then forced himself to relax his fingers. He had no doubt that Sterling was deliberately baiting him, seeking any excuse to call security back into this office and to see him escorted out of the building. He would not give the man the satisfaction.

"Luckily for you, I'm not the piece of crap you think I am. Look, we both love Angela. We both want her to be happy. I know that, as her husband, I can make her happy. I want to devote the rest of my life to her."

"And why should I believe you?"

"Because you can see it's true. I'm here, aren't I? I'm extending an olive branch. Deep down, you know Angela loves me, too. Despite everything you've ever done to try to turn her away from me. But I won't stand between the two of you, not the way you're standing between her and me. I loved her enough to let her go, but not having her in my life isn't fair to either of us. Now I'm telling you I love her enough to make a deal with you. If you agree to stand aside and stop trying to influence Angela against me, I will deed the land that her grandfather willed to me to her on our marriage."

There, he'd laid his trump card on the table.

"Obviously," he continued, "I would have preferred you to bestow your blessing on our relationship without what some may see as a bribe, but I prefer to look at it as an act of good faith. And Angela, well, she can make of it what she may. I'm sure you would rather your daughter see you through eyes that aren't clouded by the thought that you only gave us your blessing because it meant, in the long run, your family would get their hands back on land you've always considered should have been yours and Tamara's.

"Look, I love your daughter with all my heart. I will be a good husband to her and a fine father to any children we might be lucky enough to have. That land will eventually become theirs. Isn't that what you want in the long run?"

Sterling leaned back in his executive chair and pressed his fingertips together, studying Ryder carefully over their steepled peaks.

"Let me think about it," he finally said.

Ryder felt himself begin to relax. As progress went, that was a start. Certainly a better position than where they'd been before he walked into Perry's office today. Perry might have conceded to think about it, but Ryder could see that his stony visage had softened. By sweetening the pot with the land he'd inherited from Tamara's father, he knew he stood a far greater chance of winning the man's support.

"Which brings me to the Texas Cattleman's Club," Ryder started.

"I wondered when you'd bring that up. Don't push me, Currin. I might consider supporting your marriage to my daughter, but I will not relinquish my pitch for control of the TCC here in Houston."

"I'm not asking you to. But I do think we need to declare a truce and actually start to work together to find the killer. On opposite sides of the boardroom table we're formidable, but think how much stronger we could be if we worked together. Both for Angela's sake and for the reputation of the Houston club."

Again, silence stretched between the two men. After a couple of minutes Sterling Perry stood and came around to where Ryder had also risen from his seat. Was this where he ejected him from his office? Ryder wondered. He didn't know who was the more surprised when Perry stuck out his hand. Ryder didn't waste a second. He took it and shook it firmly.

"Truce," Perry said.

"Truce," Ryder agreed.

Eight

Zoe paced her motel room in irritation. Still no confirmation from the sheriff's office of a day when she'd be able to interview Jesse Stevens. Royal wasn't that antiquated. Someone was stalling; they had to be. In the meantime, she had an investigation to complete. She'd spent much of the day visiting places around town, asking random questions about Mr. Stevens and how the people around here saw him. So far all she'd heard were his praises sung from the rooftops. It was starting to get on her last nerve. No one was that perfect.

She'd begun to think she'd be better off hauling him back to Houston and questioning him there, but she knew if she did that, she'd likely get offside with Sheriff Battle, and she'd been at this long enough to know that you needed all the friends and solid contacts you could get. You never knew when you might need to call in a favor. So that left her cooling her heels, wondering what the heck to do next.

Take up horse riding? A course in cattle branding, perhaps? Both ideas made her skin crawl.

Zoe reached for her laptop and fired it up, scrolling again through the case notes she had on Vincent Hamm. It had all been so convincing, the way he'd left work after bitching about his job for weeks and vocally dreaming of a life in the Caribbean, spending his days surfing, then virtually disappearing into thin air before sending a text from the British Virgin Islands. But she knew he couldn't possibly have sent that text. Then who'd done it?

For a guy who had no enemies, he still managed to end up dead. Instinct told her it had to be connected to the building where he was found—the proposed Texas Cattleman's Club in Houston. But then there was this message from Jesse Stevens on Hamm's phone. As far as she knew, Stevens had nothing to do with the new club, but maybe there was a link she was missing here. Someone had tracked Hamm to the building. Was it Stevens? The crimescene pictures were useless. After the flooding there'd been little chance of retrieving what could have been vital evidence. The forensic examination of his body by the medical examiner had also yielded very little, besides a grossly bloated body with its face gone.

"Argh!" she groaned out loud and closed her computer.

Maybe a run would clear her head. She glanced at her watch and decided she had time before getting ready for tonight. Across the room the garment bag hanging on the door of the cupboard that passed as a wardrobe in this place caught her eye. She'd splashed out on the new dress specifically with Cord's reaction to it very firmly in her mind. Together with the skinny-heeled black patent leather pumps, the emerald green cocktail dress with its plunging neckline was bound to excite him. Heck, it had excited her just trying it on in the store. And teamed with the green-

and-white crystal necklace she'd bought to go with it, and the white crystal studs the sales girl had told her were the perfect accompaniment to the outfit, she knew she'd knock his eyes out.

She thought for a second of how much she'd spent. Almost a month's salary. And for a guy? Someone she'd known, what, two days? She had to be mad. But that ever-present tingle that took over her body every time she thought of him reasserted itself, reminding her that this wasn't just about pleasing him or seeking his approval. It was about pleasing herself, too. She wanted to look good. So what if it wasn't the kind of outfit she'd wear to a family barbecue, which was pretty much the sum total of her social life. There'd be other men, other dates.

As soon as she thought of it, she pushed the idea out of her head. She didn't have time for dating. Not now. Not when a murderer still roamed free. But a dalliance with a handsome rancher? Yeah, she thought, smiling to herself as she subconsciously reached out to stroke the garment bag, she could squeeze that in.

Feeling as though she'd fooled herself into total justification for her shopping spree, Zoe changed into her running gear and slipped out of the motel, locking the door firmly behind her. An hour ought to do it, and maybe it'd help wear off the edge of sexual hunger that constantly badgered her every time she thought about Cord Galicia.

She was wrong. Two hours wouldn't have even been enough. Even though she'd pushed herself hard in the early evening heat, after returning to her room she still had that crazy itchy feeling that she knew only Cord Galicia could scratch. She was losing her grip. Normally at this stage of a case she'd be 100 percent focused on the job—no distractions. And yet with this one—and very possibly because there was so little to go on—she was all too easily distracted.

Maybe she ought to call Cord and cancel their arrangements for tonight. She even got as far as pulling his number up on her phone, but as her finger hovered over the call command, she backed out of the app and put her phone back down again. She groaned out loud and stomped one foot in frustration. She couldn't do it. She wanted to see him tonight. There, she admitted it.

Groaning again at her weakness for a man she should never have hooked up with, Zoe went through to the cramped bathroom and stripped off her running gear before stepping under the cool spray. She sucked in a sharp breath as the water hit her overheated body and goose bumps rose on her skin. It took a couple of minutes before the water came up to temperature, and it gave her time to get her thoughts in order and her raging libido under control.

Normally she'd be fine at this stage of a relationship. She snorted as she squirted some shampoo into her hand and massaged the liquid through her short, thick hair. Relationship? No way this was anything approaching that kind of serious. Besides, she didn't do serious. Didn't want to. Not yet, anyway. She had several more notches she wanted to achieve on the metaphorical belt that was her career with Houston P.D. She'd made it this far without distraction; she didn't plan on derailing her momentum any time soon.

Zoe rinsed out the shampoo and applied conditioner before using shower gel to wash herself clean of the grime she'd picked up during her run. Half an hour in one direction and she'd been out of town in open space. Sure, there'd been signs of civilization, like fences and the occasional car, but overall, there'd been a sense of openness and calm that she'd never felt before. Running in her neighborhood in Houston was always risky. Whether it was traffic or other sidewalk users, she always had to have her wits about her. She came home satisfied with the physical outlet but less mentally fulfilled than she felt today. Maybe the country had something to recommend it after all. Not that she'd ever live here, not with her work in Houston. But visit from time to time? Yeah, she could do that.

As she dried herself off and blew out her hair, tousling it with her fingers, she thought about her family. They'd hooted with laughter when she'd told them where she was heading, knowing how citified she was. And her sisters-in-law had chuckled alongside her brothers in total agreement. While Zoe loved the fact that her brothers had met their perfect matches, and that her parents were still incredibly happy together, she did wonder sometimes if she'd find that level of contentment herself.

When she thought about her future, contentment never really factored in, anyway. It was all about drive and progress and promotion. At a certain point, though, she'd have to stop, unless she wanted to find herself chief of police one day. She smirked at her reflection as she smoothed on some tinted moisturizer and dusted it with a light coating of powder. Her? Chief of police? She'd never handle the politics or the glad-handing required. But she wouldn't mind, one day, finding the balance between work and play and settling down with that special someone.

Her parents had fallen in love in high school and married the day after graduation. Her brothers had waited until they were a little older, but each had met his future wife and known what he wanted almost immediately. None of them had wasted time on long courtships or engagements. It seemed the Warren family were all about knowing what they wanted and going for it.

She'd never found that one person that made her feel certain that he was the one. Except for Cord.

She froze, her hand midway to her eyes and the mascara wand dangling uselessly in her fingers. Where the hell was she going with this? She wasn't ready to be married. She wasn't ready to settle down. Cord had made it clear, even if he hadn't used the exact words, that he was the kind of guy that wanted a woman who was all about home and hearth and family. She was definitely not that person. She was driven by her career. By the need to bring the bad guys to justice, by the determination to see that her victims wouldn't remain victimized for the rest of their lives. That they'd have closure.

Geez, she didn't even know why she was letting her mind flow down this track. That was the trouble with having to leave the city. It left you too much damn time to think and let your mind wander down ridiculous paths that under normal circumstances you wouldn't consider at all.

Giving herself a sharp mental shake, Zoe finished applying her makeup and stepped through to the main room to take the cocktail dress from the hanger. It was nothing to look at just hanging there; in fact, she'd been very ho-hum about it when the shop assistant had suggested it to her. But when she'd put it on, it was transformed—and it transformed her right along with it. Not just her appearance, but how she felt. In this dress she felt all woman. A woman with wiles.

The deep V of the neckline made wearing a bra impossible, and due to the silkiness of the fabric Zoe had accepted the suggestion she wear nipple covers with the outfit. Given her company for the night, and the way he made her feel, she thought she'd spare the rest of the restaurant the evidence of her perpetual desire for Cord Galicia. She chuckled as she put the things on, then slipped on a skin-toned thong before putting on the dress.

She smoothed it over her hips, then reached for the jewelry she'd bought to go with it. Finally she slid her feet into her shoes and picked up the small evening bag she'd bought to complete the ensemble. She went back into the bathroom to check her reflection in the floor-length mirror behind the door and barely recognized the creature who stared back at her.

A knock at her motel room door made her move away from the mirror and the stranger she'd seen there. Was this what seeing someone like Cord was doing to her? Changing her into someone she no longer identified with? But it was still her beneath the figure-hugging emerald green dress and the hair and makeup. Just a different her. And there was no reason why this version of herself couldn't have free rein right now, was there?

She swung the door open and felt her heart skitter in her chest at the sight of the man standing there waiting for her. Dressed all in black, from his boots to his shirt and jacket, and wearing a stunning silver-and-turquoise bolo tie, Cord looked about as dark and mysterious as a man could get. Until he smiled and her new lover shone through under his frank appreciation as his eyes skimmed her from head to foot and back again.

"Wow. You look amazing."

"Thank you. You look very nice, too," she answered and stepped through the door, making sure it was locked behind her.

"Nice? I'll have you know I went to a great deal of effort for you tonight."

His tone sounded wounded, but there was no doubt he was teasing her. It was another of the things she enjoyed about being with him. Nothing was too serious. Even when making love they could joke with each other.

"And I appreciate that," she said, patting him on the chest before fingering the bolo. "I especially like this."

"It was my grandfather's. I think he'd have liked you. He enjoyed the company of strong women."

Zoe felt a sense of accomplishment at the compliment. Sure, she knew that Cord found her sexually attractive, but underneath all that she'd sensed a reserve—as if she wasn't quite the kind of woman he wanted but, for the same reasons that drew her to him, he simply couldn't resist her.

"C'mon," he said, taking her by the hand. "Let's go."

The warmth of his skin permeated her own, sending that intriguing buzz of electrical current through her as they walked to his car. She took a step back.

"This is yours?"

She gestured to the sleek and shiny low-slung black Maserati that graced the parking lot next to her own dusty vehicle.

"Like it?" he asked before opening the passenger door and holding it for her.

"It's beautiful. I had no idea you had something like this. I was expecting the truck."

Cord smiled in response. "A beautiful woman deserves a beautiful form of transport."

He closed the door and went around to his side of the car. They completed the journey out to the Texas Cattleman's Club mostly in silence, but it didn't feel awkward. Cord had reached across and taken her hand, resting it beneath his own on his thigh as he drove. She enjoyed the intimacy of the action about as much as she enjoyed the man sitting beside her.

"So, the food is good here?" she commented as they

arrived out front of the club and pulled up next to the car valet who'd stepped forward. "It looks popular."

"*Popular* is an understatement. This place is a part of the fabric of Royal."

He put a hand to the small of her back and guided her through the front door.

Cord couldn't believe his self-restraint. Seeing Zoe framed in the doorway of her motel room dressed like she'd stepped off the cover of some glossy European fashion magazine had forced him to call on every ounce of gentlemanlike behavior to prevent himself from walking her straight back into the room and closing the door behind them. All he'd wanted to do in that instant was lose himself in her, and the truth of that frightened him. Sure, he'd started this in an attempt to keep her distracted and away from Jesse while he tended to Janet. But right now Cord couldn't say his motives were entirely philanthropic. In fact, they were the complete opposite.

Even now, with his hand against the small of her back as they entered the club, he was fighting with the base urge to turn her right around and back out to the car and take her home again. He wasn't in the mood for polite company and the conversation that he knew being seen with a woman here tonight would engender. What the hell had he been thinking?

"Mr. Galicia, good to see you this evening. Your table is ready. Please, come with me," the maître d' said as they entered the restaurant.

Cord let his hand drop from Zoe's back and gestured for her to follow the maître d' while he kept a circumspect two paces behind her. All the better to see the delicious curves of her butt in that dress, his alter ego reminded him. He clamped down on the thought but not before he felt the

ripple of arousal the view before him wrought. The food
tonight was going to have to be spectacular to distract
him from what seeing her in that dress did to him. And
the shoes… He felt another ripple shudder through him.
Those heels were seriously sexy. He wondered, briefly,
if she'd keep them on later for him, if he asked real nice.

You're not doing yourself any favors, he growled at himself. He watched as Zoe was seated at the table and felt a
somewhat feral burst of protectiveness as the maître d's
gaze lingered a second too long on Zoe's exposed cleav-
age as he shook out her napkin and laid it across her lap.
Forcing himself to uncurl the fingers that had instinctively
formed into fists, he took his seat and listened with half
an ear as the man told them he'd send their waiter along
shortly.

"Nice place," Zoe said, looking around.

"I'm sure you've seen similar in Houston," he said a
little flatly.

Somehow seeing the way that guy had stared at Zoe had
taken a little of the shine off the evening for him. In fact,
he was beginning to question what he'd been thinking inviting her here. Showing off? Letting the city girl know
he could give her as good as she was used to? *Idiot*, he told
himself. They weren't even a couple in the true sense of
the word. He had no right to feel possessive about her, no
matter how intimately he knew her body.

"Not quite as sumptuous as this," she said with a smile
and took a sip from her water glass.

The wine waiter came across and took their orders,
shortly followed by the waiter bringing menus and letting them know the specials. Cord was grateful for the re-
spite when they took their time selecting their appetizers
and mains, and a little surprised, too, when he discovered
they'd each chosen the same.

"Great minds think alike, hmm?" Zoe said with a warm smile that sent a wave of lust straight to his groin.

"Fools seldom differ," he countered, still a little surly.

Zoe reached across the table and took his hand. "Is everything okay? Would you rather we left?"

He shook his head. Of course she'd notice his change in mood. She was trained to observe these sorts of things. To study the human condition and ascertain the difference between the truth and the lies. Was that what she was doing with him all the time? Did she realize that while he'd started using sex as a distraction tactic, it had quickly become something else that he didn't want to define? He realized she was waiting for an answer and gave her fingers a squeeze.

"No, it's nothing. It's been a while since I've dined here is all."

In fact, the last time he'd eaten here was when he proposed to Britney, just before she left for training. The memory made his heart ache. Just two short years ago and yet it felt like a lifetime. And here he was, overlaying a new memory. He didn't know whether to be annoyed with himself or pleased that he was finally letting go. One thing was for sure, though—this thing with Zoe wouldn't go any further than the time she was here in Royal. He'd make sure of it. He couldn't handle the constant fear of living with a woman who carried a gun for a living again. His worst nightmare had already been realized once; there was no way he was tempting fate again.

The food, when it came, was sublime, and there was something inherently sensuous about the way Zoe enjoyed her food. He found he took pleasure in watching her, listening to the cadence of her voice as they talked, simply enjoying her presence. The last of his bad mood brushed away, and they were lingering over coffee and sharing a truly delicate serving of crème brûlée when he became aware of someone stopping beside their table.

"Cord, darling, how are you? We haven't seen you here in ages."

Cord rose to his feet, identifying one of his mother's Women's Institute cronies and her long-suffering husband hovering right behind her.

"Mrs. Radison, good to see you looking so well."

"Oh, you charmer, you. I received an email from your mom the other day. Seems like they're enjoying Palm Springs. And who is this?"

Just like that, the woman dispensed with the niceties and got straight to the point that he knew had led her to stop at his table. He had no doubt that the fact he'd been out with a new woman would be all around the gossips in town within five minutes of Olive Radison leaving the building. She put the word *social* in capital letters when it came to social media.

"Zoe Warren, please meet Olive Radison and her husband, Bert," Cord said, hoping this encounter would be over soon.

"Pleased to meet you, dear," Olive Radison purred. "So lovely to see Cord moving on. After all, it's been a while now, hasn't it, dear?" She patted Cord gently on the cheek, oblivious to the way his body had stiffened as if set in concrete. "Come along, Bert. We mustn't keep these young people from enjoying one another's company any longer."

And then she was gone, leaving behind a generous waft of her floral fragrance and a sense of discomfort settling on Cord's shoulders like a leaden cloak.

"Sorry about that. One of my mom's friends."

"No problem. She seemed friendly," Zoe commented lightly.

But there was something there in her gaze now that

wasn't there before. Questions that remained unasked and, on his part, unanswered. Suddenly he couldn't wait to get out of here.

"You done?" he asked abruptly.

Zoe's eyes flicked to his, and she stared at him a moment before giving him a quick nod. "Sure," she answered, gathering up her bag and rising from her chair. "I'll just go to the bathroom. Be back in a minute."

The dessert sat on the table, still unfinished, just like so many other things between them, he thought as he gestured for the bill. He'd settled the account by the time she returned to the dining room, and he rose to meet her halfway across the room. Together they went out to wait for the valet to bring his car around. The trip back to her motel felt a whole lot longer than the journey out. It was only as they neared the motel that they saw the flash of red lights and saw the fire engines and hoses lining the street.

"What the hell?" Zoe cried out as it became apparent it was the motel that had been on fire.

Cord pulled over and together they approached the area where the motel manager had assembled with a few of the occupants.

"What's going on?" Zoe asked when the woman turned to her to give her attention.

"I'm sorry, hon. But it seems someone's phone charger started a fire in the end unit. Once it took hold in the roof it spread quickly. There are fire walls between the units, but even so, there is a lot of smoke and water damage. I'm not sure they'll be allowing anyone back in to stay tonight. We'll have to reassess in the morning."

"Our things? Can we retrieve them?"

"I'll speak to the fire chief when he's free, okay, hon? Have you got somewhere else you can stay tonight?"

"She's staying with me," Cord said firmly.

"Thank goodness," the manager said with obvious relief. "The other motel near here is closed for renovations,
and the hotel in town is able to put up a few people, but
they're almost at capacity themselves, so we're short of
beds."

Cord felt Zoe shiver as the manager moved away to
where it looked like a command center had been established. He identified the fire chief there, and Nate Battle,
too.

"My weapon is in there and my computer. I have to
be able to clear my things from my room safe," Zoe said
firmly. "I should go and speak to the sheriff."

That cold slice of reality cut through him again. Every
time he let himself relax a little, forget a little, that one
piece of hell-no-don't-go-there would come back and
smack him clean in the face.

"Let's wait a bit. You're a registered guest. They know
you're here. They'll come to us when they can," he said.
"Are you warm enough?"

Before she could answer, he shrugged off his jacket and
laid it around her shoulders. He could see she was at the
point of protesting but thankfully she didn't. The night air
was cooler than it had been, and she sure wasn't dressed
for the climate.

It was another hour before the fire crew deemed it safe
for those in units farthest from the burned-out room to
enter their rooms and retrieve their belongings. Zoe didn't
waste a second. Cord went with her, packing her toiletries in the bathroom as she grabbed her small case and
her gun and laptop.

"This it?" he asked as he came through from the bathroom.

She gave him a brusque nod.

"You sure pack light."

"I wasn't planning on staying long."

Cord felt a twinge of guilt at her comment. She would be staying a whole lot longer now, thanks to him and his little discussion with Frank.

"Hey, don't worry about it. At least you know you can stay at my place."

"Your ranch is hardly the hub of activity here in Royal. What if I get bored?"

She gave him a challenging look.

"Then it will be up to me, as your host, to ensure you don't get bored, won't it? C'mon, let's go. The stink of this place is getting right up my nose."

Zoe followed the Maserati out to the ranch. She didn't want to be stranded when the call came to say she could conduct the interview with Stevens, and she couldn't see Cord letting her use the Maserati, although the idea had merit.

She pulled her car up outside Cord's house, swinging it off to one side of the driveway as he turned toward the multibay garage to the side of the property. He met her at the steps to the front door.

"You could have parked in the garage," he suggested.

"I prefer to be parked for a quick getaway," she said, only half joking.

He snorted, and she could see he wasn't entirely pleased with her response. *Well, so what*, she thought. This evening had gone from a very promising beginning to crash and, quite literally, burn in a very short space of time. And, she noticed as they entered the house, she had managed to get soot on her new dress into the bargain. There'd better be a decent dry cleaner in town.

She fought back a yawn. With last night's lack of sleep and the drama this evening, she felt exhausted.

"You want your own room this time?" Cord asked as they went up the stairs.

"Sure," she said, annoyed that he'd offered.

Something had crawled under his skin tonight, but she was too tired and irritated to try to figure it out. He showed her into a large room that, come morning, would be bathed in sunshine. The white bed linens reminded her of her somewhat-grimy state. Despite the fact the fire hadn't reached her unit, the soot and smoke had managed to permeate everything she'd touched or brushed against.

"Thanks," she said abruptly as Cord showed her the door to the connecting bathroom. "I can manage from here."

He stopped directly in front of her. "Are you sure about that? You look done in, and—" he paused to sniff "—your stuff smells of smoke."

She groaned in frustration. "I'd better put my stuff through the wash before bed."

"Don't worry about it. Leave it with me. Go." He tugged the bag from her hands and pushed her gently in the direction of the bathroom. "Shower. I'll leave something for you to sleep in on the bed."

He was gone before she could protest. All he'd left her with was her laptop case and her toiletries bag. Her gun was tucked into the side of the computer bag, and she'd seen his gaze flick past it. It was obvious he had some aversion to her carrying a weapon. Odd, when Texas was an open carry state. It wasn't unusual to see any adult carrying a gun. But, she'd noticed, he didn't carry one himself. She shrugged, putting the thought aside for now.

The shower was everything she longed for. She let the hot water sluice over her body and wash away the tension of the evening. What had that all been about, anyway? Something from Cord's past, obviously. And, just as obviously, something he hadn't wanted to discuss. Maybe she could probe a little more about that tomorrow, but for now, she needed rest.

She toweled off and padded through to the bedroom on bare feet. Cord had been back in here, she noticed. The drapes had been drawn and a deliciously soft T-shirt had been laid on the bed. She picked up the garment and held it to her face, inhaling the faint scent of his cologne. It felt sinfully wicked letting the wash-worn cotton skim over her body, almost like a lover's caress. And just like that, weariness fled from her body and a sensual tug of longing infused her instead.

He'd turned down her bed while she'd been showering, and she eyed the crisp white sheets with a mix of longing and aversion. It would take only a moment to head down the hallway to his room. She shook her head and yanked the sheets back a little farther. No, she was being strong. He'd clouded her mind quite enough for the very short time she'd known him. She needed to take charge of herself again.

She slid into bed and tugged the comforter up to her chin and lay there as stiff as a board, staring at the ceiling. It wasn't more than a half hour when she heard a soft knock at her bedroom door. It was so soft that if she'd been asleep, she probably wouldn't have heard it.

"Yeah," she called out.

The door opened a crack. From the soft light of the hallway she saw Cord standing there, his torso naked and a pair of pajama pants barely clinging to his hips.

"Everything okay?" he asked.

"I can't get to sleep," she admitted.

"Need some company?"

"Sure."

He was crossing the room before the word was fully

spoken, and she felt him get into the bed beside her. A few seconds later and his strong arms had pulled her against him, her back to his front. She felt him kiss the top of her shoulder where his T-shirt had fallen away to expose her skin.

"Go to sleep now," he said softly.

And, to her surprise, she did.

Nine

Zoe woke the next morning feeling like she'd had the best rest in a very long time. She rolled over to greet Cord, but he was already gone, and his side of the bed was cold, too, alerting her to the fact he'd been up for some time. Well, this was a working ranch, she reminded herself as she headed to the bathroom. When she came out, she was at a loss for what to wear and ended up staying in the T-shirt of Cord's that she'd slept in.

She made her way back downstairs and went to the kitchen, drawn by the aroma of freshly made coffee. Her mouth was quite literally watering by the time she found a mug in the cupboard and poured a cup from the carafe on the warmer.

"Good morning."

A voice from behind her made her spin around.

"Good morning to you, too. Good coffee, thanks," she answered, holding her mug up to Cord in a toast. "You're a man of surprising talents."

He smiled, the action sending a punch of heat straight through her body and making her all too aware that she stood here before him dressed in nothing but an oversize T-shirt. For all that it covered her butt and skimmed her thighs, she knew her nipples had to be prominent against the well-washed white cotton. She hazarded a glance downward. Yup, there they were. Perky as all get-out and happy as hell to see him.

And he was a sight this morning. Dressed in blue jeans, worn in all the right places, and a loose-fitting chambray shirt that was open a few buttons at the neck, he was a visual feast. Zoe took a sip of her coffee, sucking down the hot brew as if it wasn't burning the roof of her mouth and scalding her throat. Anything to distract herself from taking those few short steps across the kitchen and jumping up into Cord's arms and hooking her legs around his waist.

"Speaking of talents," he said as he grabbed a mug and poured himself a coffee, too. "Your clothes are dry and ready for you when you want to get dressed."

He made it sound as though getting dressed was optional, and for a moment she considered tormenting him by just hanging out in his T-shirt all day long. But she knew she would be the one to suffer. Already she felt as though she was at a disadvantage.

"Thanks, I'll grab them now."

"Would you like to look around the ranch with me today? I need to check some fences in the outer pastures."

"On horseback?" she asked, barely suppressing a shudder.

Sure, she could see the value of horses in this environment, but nothing and no one said she'd ever have to ride one. As far as she could tell, one end bit and the other kicked. She wasn't interested in what came in between.

"Not keen?"

"Not on horses, no. Got bikes?"

"I'm sure you'll enjoy what I'm planning. Why don't you get dressed, then we can have breakfast and get going."

"Yes, sir," she said with a mock salute. "Question."

"Yeah?"

"Where's the laundry room?"

He chuckled and pointed down a hallway off the kitchen she hadn't been down before. "Down there. You'll find it."

"Thanks."

She grabbed her things and went up to her room to dress. In no time she was back in the kitchen. She moaned out loud at the scent of breakfast cooking.

"Are those huevos rancheros?"

"Yup," Cord said, sliding eggs onto the plated tortillas topped with fried beans.

He spooned fresh salsa over the eggs and then crumbled feta cheese over the top and garnished it all with chopped cilantro. He took their plates over to the large wooden kitchen table and set them down.

"Eat," he said simply and gestured for her to take a seat.

Zoe didn't waste another second. She sampled the breakfast and moaned again.

"This is amazing. I think you must have missed your calling. Ranching? Forget it. You should have been a chef."

Cord smiled in return. "I did think about learning to cook professionally, but I was born to this ranch and its way of life. From the day I was old enough to walk, I was out there with my dad learning the ropes from the ground up, the way he learned from his dad."

"And the way you'll teach your children one day, too?"

He stiffened, his fork halfway to his mouth. "Maybe," he admitted before letting his fork clatter down onto his plate. "What about you? Planning to have kids one day?"

She shrugged, not entirely comfortable with the conversation being turned back to her. "Maybe," she replied, mimicking his answer. "But the cooking? This is seriously good. If you ever decide to give up ranching, you could make a killing with your food."

Cord helped himself to a little more salsa from the bowl he'd put on the table.

"They're my grandmother's recipes. I'll be sure to tell her you're impressed."

"Please do. This is feta cheese, right?"

Cord nodded.

"I've never been a fan of it before, but this tastes divine," Zoe enthused.

"I make it myself. I keep a few goats and like to dabble in new ideas. Who knows, maybe one day I can expand my herd some more and turn the goats and the cheese into a more commercial operation."

"Seems I learn something new about you every day," Zoe commented as she cleaned up her plate with the last scrap of a tortilla.

Cord shrugged. "I'm not complicated. If you want to know anything about me, just ask."

Zoe leaned back in her chair and looked at him. "What went wrong last night?"

"With the fire?"

"No." She pushed. "Before that. You were all good until we got to the club, and then when that woman stopped by, it was like you had been frozen in ice."

"Old memories."

Zoe waited for him to expand on that, but it seemed he felt that was quite enough on the subject because he abruptly rose from the table and cleared their plates away. Zoe rose to help him but he shooed her off.

"Go do whatever it is you women do before going out.

We'll be leaving in about fifteen minutes. Meet me by the garage."

Accepting she'd been summarily dismissed after touching on what was obviously a very raw subject for him, she did as he suggested and went back up to her room. After a quick trip to the bathroom she folded her clothes and stacked them in one of the empty drawers. They didn't take up a lot of room. Satisfied she'd killed enough time, she went downstairs and out to the garage. Cord was waiting by his truck. She could see he'd loaded some tools and a roll of fencing wire in the back of the truck.

As they headed down the drive Zoe asked, "Where are we going?"

"You'll see," Cord responded cryptically.

She fought back the urge to press him for more information, but they hadn't traveled more than five minutes before he turned off the road and drove toward what looked like a hangar. A wind sock hung limply at the end of what she worked out was a runway.

"You have an airport?"

"A private strip. Jesse and I share it, as it borders both our properties. We learned to fly together. He prefers to stick with fixed-wing and I prefer choppers."

"Choppers."

"Don't tell me you'd rather go horse riding?" he laughed.

"Actually, no, I wouldn't," she responded firmly. "Choppers are fine."

"So glad you approve," he teased. "Here, come and give me a hand with these."

He gave her his toolbox to carry while he grabbed the roll of fencing wire, then led the way into the hangar.

"We're going up in that?" Zoe asked, eyeing the small chopper settled on one side of the hangar.

"What, cold feet, Detective?"

"It's smaller than I'm used to, that's all."

"The Robinson R44 is perfect for around the ranch. We use it to monitor stock, find strays and check the fence lines. All sorts of things. It's highly maneuverable, so it's perfect for the kind of work we do."

"Sounds versatile."

"Oh, it is. You'll see for yourself in a few minutes."

"Where do you want this?" she asked, gesturing to the toolbox she'd set at her feet.

"I'll take it," he said, stepping toward her and picking it up with next to no effort at all.

She'd seen him naked so she knew he wasn't heavily muscled, but the man was very clearly strong. He hefted the toolbox into a compartment at the back of the chopper with ease and stacked the fencing wire in there, too, before attaching a pair of ground-handling wheels to the helicopter skids; then, grabbing hold of the back of the chopper, near the tail rotor, he tilted the machine and rolled it forward out of the hangar to the area marked on the tarmac with a large letter H.

Zoe followed, fascinated by the whole process. "I never realized it was as easy as that to move the thing."

Cord laughed. "There are all sorts of tools you can use. I prefer these," he said, gesturing to the removable wheels.

He bent down to remove them from the skids, and after stowing them away back in the hangar, he did a preflight inspection on the chopper. The sun glinted on the bright blue of the fuselage, making Zoe shield her eyes and wish she'd brought her sunglasses.

"There's a spare pair of sunglasses in the glove compartment in the truck if you need them," Cord said as he got to the end of his inspection.

"Thanks."

Zoe didn't waste any time. She went straight to the

truck and opened the glove compartment. The space was very full but she spied the sunglasses quickly and tugged them free. As she did so, a double-folded sheet of paper fell out with them. A funeral service notice, she realized. A stunningly pretty young woman smiled up at her from the front of the notice. She recognized her from a photo she'd seen at the house and assumed it was a relative. Zoe scanned the dates. The girl had died a couple of years ago. Was she the reason for the "memories" Cord had referred to? Instead of relatives, had they been a couple? Feeling as though she was prying into something intensely private, Zoe pushed the notice back into the glove compartment and swung it closed.

As she slid the glasses onto her nose and walked back toward the chopper, she thought about the young woman whose face had imprinted on her so firmly. There was something familiar about her, too, but she couldn't put her finger on when or where she'd seen her. Obviously she couldn't ask Cord. She didn't want to be accused of being nosy, for a start, but she sensed that the subject of the late Britney Collins was a sensitive one.

"Ready?" he asked as she drew closer.

"For sure. Thanks for the shades."

"No worries. I always carry spares."

Zoe's stomach lurched a little as they rose in the air and turned sharply to one side and flew away from the airfield. There was an incredible sense of freedom sitting here in this relatively small bubble and observing the ground racing away beneath them.

"All good?" Cord asked, his voice a little tinny through the headset he'd instructed her to wear.

"A-okay," she replied. "This is really cool."

He flung her another of those grins that made her toes curl. She watched as he competently handled the chopper, dipping and weaving along the contours of the land as they followed fence lines, until he found an area that looked to have been breached. He swiftly turned the chopper around, making Zoe's gut lurch again, before setting the machine down on a level patch of land.

"You do that as if you're born to it," she said after they'd exited the R44.

"I love it. There's a freedom that comes from being in the air that you don't get in a car or a truck. No matter how high performance."

She helped him carry his gear over to the breach in the fence line and watched as he competently made the repairs, handing him tools when he asked for them.

"You're good at this," he commented as she neatly packed his tools back into the box when he was done.

"I used to help my dad around home a lot. With my four older brothers, he had to do a lot of repairs," she said with a laugh.

"I can imagine. Did you enjoy growing up in a large family?"

"It has its drawbacks, but overall it's been good. My brothers are all married now and starting families of their own. It's a bit of a zoo when we all get together, but what can I say…it's family."

She stood up and stretched before leaning against one of the fence posts and surveying the land around them.

"Do you ever feel trapped by all of this?" she asked.

"Trapped? That's a strange way of looking at a large amount of space."

"Well, y'know. The responsibility you have to the land, to the herds, the people you employ. There's so much to consider every day of every month. You're never completely free of it, are you?"

He came and stood in front of her, and she could feel the warmth of his body as he came in close.

"Oh, city girl, you have no idea," he murmured before reaching up to pull something from her hair.

"Was that an insect?" she said with a wary glance at his hand as he tossed something away.

"Just a bit of grass. You're out of your element right now, aren't you?"

"It doesn't bother me," she said, defending herself.

"But you're not comfortable, either, are you?" he pressed.

"I'm never comfortable when I'm not in control. I don't know this world." She gestured around them. "Your world," she clarified.

"And you call yourself a Texan?" he teased, lowering his face to hers. "Let's see if we can't relax you a bit."

He planted his arms on the fence on either side of her and pressed his body against hers as he took her mouth in a sweeping kiss. He'd been thinking about doing this from the moment he first saw her in the kitchen this morning dressed in his old shirt. Last night had been difficult, but even so he hadn't been able to leave Zoe completely alone. He felt raw, as if his nerves were exposed and irritated, and the only thing that would soothe him would be to feel her warmth curled up against him as she slept in his arms.

That had been enough, for then. But now? Now was another story entirely. Now, with the clear fall light bathing the land around them and with the shade trees changing color and beginning to drop their leaves, the sheer satisfaction of being here in his element made him want to pull her into the spell, too.

Her mouth opened beneath his, her tongue meeting his and tasting him with the same eagerness he felt for her. It wasn't long before he knew that kissing her wasn't enough. Would likely never be enough. His desire for her was like a drug in his body, creating a need he couldn't, didn't want to control.

It was both exhilarating and terrifying in equal proportions. Look at how much he'd needed to be with her last night. Even with memories of Britney swirling in the back of his mind, he'd sought Zoe, convincing himself that she needed him more than he needed her. But as he'd lain there, holding her, listening to her steady breathing, absorbing the warmth of her skin, he'd admitted to himself that his need had been the greater.

He'd woken early, determined to put distance between them, but the second he'd seen her again all resolve had been blown to the four corners of the earth. He was glad she'd come out with him today. He'd wanted her to see this, his world, as she'd called it. To understand the call of the land, the beauty that lay before them.

What was the point, though? She was going to be here for only a short time longer. He doubted that Frank would be able to put Sheriff Battle off on the repairs to the equipment for much longer.

He'd take what he could get, he decided. Share with Zoe the perfect synchronicity of their bodies. And when she left, at least he'd have the memories.

Cord tugged her down to the ground and pulled her on top of him. He pushed his hands through her silky hair and cupped the back of her head as he continued to kiss her. She tasted so good, so right, and the way their bodies fit together was equally so.

"What's this?" Zoe asked, pulling slightly away. "Are we checking ground temperatures now?"

He laughed. She was amazing. He hadn't laughed during lovemaking this much, ever.

"Call it whatever you like. I thought it would be a shame to get your blouse all grass stained, hence me being on the bottom," he replied.

"Oh, so you don't want me to get dirty?"

There was a wicked gleam in her eye that totally undid him. "Oh yeah, get as down and dirty as you want."

"Did you bring a condom?"

"Do I look like the kind of man who'd forget something as important as that?"

She cocked her head and grinned. "I'm so glad you like to think of everything."

And then all sensible thought fled as she yanked his buttons undone and bared his chest. Her fingers spread over his skin, her nails lightly rasping over his nipples and sending shocks of delight through his body. He lay there, allowing her access to every part of him, lifting his hips in acquiescence as she tugged his belt free and undid his jeans. When her hands closed over his erection, he jerked against her.

"Whoa, there, cowboy," she murmured. "In some kind of hurry?"

"In some kind of something," he muttered in return.

He clenched his teeth and tensed as she stroked him, her rhythm perfect, and when she wriggled lower down his legs and took him into her mouth, he all but lost it. She licked and tasted him, drawing him into her mouth, then letting him slide free, in a tantalizing, teasing dance. The light breeze was a delicious cold shock against his wet skin. He couldn't take much more of this. He wanted—no, *needed*—to be inside her.

"Condom, front right pocket," he rasped.

Thankfully she was in agreement, because in a matter of moments she'd sheathed him and was pushing her jeans down and standing only briefly enough to remove them and her panties before lowering herself over him again. He could feel the heat at her center as she hovered over him, then reached for his shaft, guiding it to her entrance. And when she slid the rest of the way down he surged upward, meeting her halfway, again and again until the blue sky above them blurred and the only sounds he could hear were their labored breathing and the slap of their skin as she rode him to completion.

She sprawled across his body and he could feel the race of her heartbeat against his chest. He wrapped his arms around her, holding her close, knowing that this was only temporary but wishing it could be so much more. It was at least a half hour later that he felt her shift.

"We'll make a cowgirl of you yet," he teased as she got up and started to tug her clothes back on.

"Certainly has a few highlights to recommend it," she responded just as lightly.

But he could see the shadow that passed across her face. Yes, she was equally as aware as he was that what they shared was transitory. Well, given that fact, there was only one thing for it. They had to make the most of the time they had available.

And he did. Over the next three days he took her everywhere around the ranch with him, even going so far as to getting her up on his oldest, gentlest mare for a rein-led walk. And every night they lost themselves in each other. Of course, he never forgot who and what she was. Not even for a minute. Hard to when she checked her messages daily for updates on the Hamm case and spent a good portion of each evening on her computer. And there was her ever-present handgun. She hadn't worn it that first day they'd gone out in the chopper, but he couldn't avoid seeing its bulk nestled under her blouse every day since.

For now, he felt as though they were living in a bubble,

one where the outside world couldn't get to them. Which was just the way he liked it. Jesse had told him that Janet was coming home from the hospital this week—the infection she'd developed when her appendix burst was now almost clear. By the time she was firmly back on the road to recovery, and Jesse was relieved of the concerns he'd suffered on his baby sister's behalf, hopefully Zoe would have lost the bee in her bonnet about his best friend's possible involvement in the murder case.

He should have known better.

Ten

Zoe had taken control of the kitchen, with Cord supervising her breakfast-cooking skills. It was hard to focus with him standing there, leaning against the kitchen countertop with his hair still damp from the shower they'd just had together. Granted, he was dressed, which should have reduced the impact he had on her senses even after these past few days staying together. But to Zoe's surprise, her interest in Cord Galicia didn't appear to be waning anytime soon. In fact, the longer she stayed here, the harder she found it to focus on her case.

She was just removing bacon from the grill when Cord's cell phone trilled in his pocket.

"It's my dad," he said, checking the screen. "I need to take this."

"No worries, I'll keep everything warm for you."

"Everything?" he asked, stealing a quick kiss from her already swollen lips.

"Go, answer your phone call!" she laughed, giving him a playful shove.

She could hear him talking in the living room. Heard the sincerity and love in his voice as he spoke with his father. The bond was strong there, she realized. It surprised her in some ways, because Cord seemed to be so very self-contained. Not needing anyone or anything.

Zoe broke eggs into the pan and added cream, dill and seasoning before scrambling them all together with a spatula. She was just ladling them out onto warmed plates when the house phone started to ring.

"Can you get that please?" Cord called from the other room.

"Sure," Zoe replied and lifted the handset from the station in the kitchen. "Galicia residence."

"Is Cord available?"

"I'm sorry, he's on another call. Can I take a message?"

"Sure, it's Frank. Can you tell him I can't delay the repair of the sound and video equipment any longer? Nate's getting antsy and I really don't want to be in the sheriff's bad books. Tell Cord we're square now. I put it off as long as I could."

Zoe's brow furrowed in a frown. "Did you say sound and video equipment?"

"Yeah, yeah. Cord will know what I'm talking about. Can you just see he gets the message?"

"Oh, I'll see he gets the message, all right," she answered before severing the call.

Anger rose inside her like a storm surge, filling every nook and cranny of her mind and her body until it seeped from her pores like a palpable presence in the room. She replayed the conversation she'd just had over and over in her head. Each time it remained the same. Each time the result was damning. Cord had tampered with her investigation by deliberately delaying her interview with Jesse Stevens.

She heard a sound behind her and wheeled as Cord came back into the kitchen.

"Sorry about that. My dad sure can talk. He's missing the ranch." He came and stood beside her. "Hey, something's wrong. What's up?"

"You tell me," she said tightly.

"What do you mean? Who was on the phone?"

"Your friend Frank."

She watched his face as understanding dawned. "Ah."

Cord's expression closed up. Gone was the loving, playful cowboy who had occupied her days, and her nights. In place was the silent, careful man who'd greeted her the day she'd arrived in Royal.

"What you did was illegal. You deliberately hindered my investigation," she said bitingly through clenched teeth. "I should arrest you for that."

"Are you going to?"

"No. I don't plan to waste another second on you. Besides, the paperwork would be more than you're worth."

She shoved past him and headed upstairs. He was behind her a split second later.

"Where are you going?"

"To do my job."

She stormed into his bedroom, which they'd been sharing since that day out in the chopper, grabbed her bag and started throwing her things into it. Cord didn't try to stop her. Didn't so much as step in her way. She didn't know what upset her more—the fact he'd done what he had, or the fact that he didn't seem to care now that she knew. Then understanding dawned.

She wheeled to face him, hands fisted and planted on her hips.

"This was your intention all along, wasn't it?" she demanded. "Keep me distracted so I wouldn't question your buddy!"

To her utter humiliation he didn't say a word, but she saw the truth in his eyes.

"You bastard!" she spat.

She snatched her bag from the bed and hammered down the stairs. She paused only long enough to grab her laptop and case from the sitting room and then she was out the door. He didn't follow. He never said a word. And as bitter, angry tears started to track down her cheeks, she realized she'd been taken for a complete fool. Seduced by an oh-so-talented lover. Falling for all the stereotypes she'd sworn she'd never be caught by. Turned out she was just as fallible as anyone else. Worse, she'd been as stupid as some of her colleagues had always expected her to be. She'd lost sight of the case and all because a handsome man had paid her attention.

Well, she thought as she swiped the tears from her face and turned her car toward town, she'd learned her lesson, hadn't she? This interview with Jesse Stevens was happening today, one way or another, and then she was heading home.

She drove directly to the sheriff's office and parked outside. Thankfully Sheriff Battle was in when she asked for him, and he was quick to assure her that the interview room would be ready for her early in the afternoon. He also offered to contact Jesse himself and ask the guy to come in. All of which meant she had a few hours to cool her heels before she could complete her task here and then get the hell out of town.

Zoe headed to the Daily Grind and grabbed a coffee and something to eat. As she sat at the small table near the window and stared outside, she wondered if Cord had eaten the breakfast she'd just finished preparing before the scales had been torn from her eyes. Darn, but she'd been such an idiot. If anything, that hurt more than his lack of sincerity in starting their affair. And, yes, he'd started it. And she'd let him.

She suppressed the tingle that began in her body at the memory of that first night, of being pressed against the motel room door while he did incredible things to her. It had all been fake. A distraction tactic. And it had worked. But no more. She didn't trust anyone, especially not Cord Galicia.

Her mobile phone pinged with a text confirming the interview with Jesse Stevens at one o'clock. She texted back her agreement and finished her coffee. She still had hours to kill. Realizing she needed to burn off some steam, Zoe went for a long walk. While she walked, her phone buzzed. She looked at the screen. Cord. Damn him. She declined the call and shoved the phone back into her pocket, where it began buzzing again. She ignored it, only to have the darn thing continue to go off at regular intervals. In the end she turned off her phone, but she'd worked up a fine head of steam by the time she was shown into the interview room at the station. Sheriff Battle was already there, setting up the equipment. He looked up, his expression growing wary as she walked in.

"You okay?" he asked.

"I'm fine," she said sharply, then sighed. "No, actually I'm not fine, but my day will improve once I get this interview done and get back to Houston."

"Sick of us already?"

She cracked a wry grin. "I do have a job to do. Seems everyone has forgotten that fact."

Nate Battle shrugged. "Looked like you were getting

real comfortable with Cord the other night when he took you back to his place."

She stiffened. "He put me up for a few days, that's all."

He stared at her for a few moments, then nodded briefly. "Jesse should be here any minute. The recording equipment will upload a digital file to your email address when we're done. It'll be waiting for you when you get home."

"Good," she said. "Nice to know it's all working fine now."

"Yeah, about that…"

"Don't worry about it. The problem's sorted."

Yes, the problem was sorted, and she'd begun to accept that she'd had a narrow escape from a dirty, low-down snake. It would have been all too easy to fall for Cord Galicia. She'd deeply enjoyed her time with him on the ranch, had even begun to see the beauty that held him there, although her craving for hot asphalt and skyscrapers still lingered beneath the surface. She shook her head slightly. Nope, she wasn't going back down that memory track. She'd seal it up instead, for good.

A sound at the door made her turn and watch as one of the sheriff's deputies showed Jesse Stevens into the room.

"Good afternoon, y'all," he said, removing his hat and setting it on the desk between them.

Nate Battle didn't waste any time. He launched straight into the formalities, inviting both Jesse and Zoe to take a seat and then turning on the equipment and making the introductory statement for the record. Zoe felt her skin itch as she waited her turn to fire the questions she'd been hanging out to ask. After confirming it was Jesse's voice on Hamm's phone, she pushed him a little harder.

"You were extremely angry with Mr. Hamm when you left that message, weren't you?"

"I was."

Jesse's response was clipped, and she saw the glint of irritation in his green eyes.

"Could you state for the recording why you were angry with Mr. Hamm?"

"Sure. It's common knowledge that over the years I did several favors for the guy. When the shoe was on the other foot and I asked him for help getting an internship at Perry Holdings for my sister, he flat out refused. Seems the big city and his job there made him think he was too good for his old friends back home."

"I can see why that would have upset you," she said, baiting him.

"Upset me, yes. But not enough to murder the guy. I did not kill Vincent Hamm. I was mad at him, for sure, but I took it on the chin and moved on. I told you that around the time they say he was murdered I was three hours away from Houston, attending a stock auction." He reached inside his jacket pocket and drew out a folded wad of paper. "Here," he said, unfolding the papers and stabbing them with his finger. "As requested, my receipts. Motel, gas and copies of sale agreements."

Zoe looked over at Nate, who reached for the papers and carefully scrutinized them.

"It all looks genuine," he said carefully. "Covers the three-day window of time in which Hamm's murder most likely occurred, no question."

"Of course it's genuine," Jesse interjected. "I keep telling you. I'm innocent. Look, I'm sorry the guy is dead. No one deserved to die like that, but maybe he had it coming from someone other than me. Maybe he said no to just one person too many."

"Running my investigation now, are we?" Zoe added acerbically.

"I apologize, ma'am," Jesse said. "Not my place, I know.

But stand in my shoes for a minute and think about this. I would lose my family, my home—everything—if I were guilty of what you're suggesting. Look, if those receipts aren't enough for you, let me take a polygraph. I know you have one here, Nate. Hook me up. It'll prove my innocence."

Nate looked at Zoe with a question clear in his eyes. She took her time answering. On the surface, it would seem that Jesse Stevens was telling the truth. She sighed. Another dead end.

"Sure," she said to both men. "Let's do it.

It was close to four o'clock before the sheriff walked her out to her car. A sheet of paper flapped from under one of her wiper blades.

"Are you kidding me?" she groaned when she spied the parking fine.

Nate laughed and took it from her hand. "Let me take care of it."

"Thanks," she answered and opened her car door. "And thanks for your help today. I'm sure you probably had better things to do."

He shrugged. "There's always something to do around here. Might not be the bright lights and the big city, but it's never dull. You're satisfied now that Jesse's not your man?"

She nodded—a grimace twisting her features. "Yeah, but it puts us back to square one again. I'm sorry, Sheriff. I know you made promises to Hamm's family. I'd hoped we'd be able to bring them some closure by now."

"It's okay. I know you're not going to quit on this."

"Oh, trust me. Quitting is not in my nature. Obviously I need to shift focus. I've gone over and over my notes, but there's something I'm just not seeing. I keep coming back to the crime scene. It's gotta be someone connected to the building, or maybe even to someone connected to Perry Holdings. But where are the damn clues? Hamm must have seen or heard something that had gotten him killed, so why can't I find it?"

"You will. Eventually."

She laughed, but it lacked any humor. "Yeah. Maybe it'll shake loose on the drive back."

"It's getting late. You sure you don't want to stay an extra night?"

"No, definitely not. I need to get back," she said firmly. "I've been away too long as it is."

"Sure. You know, there were a lot of people surprised to see you with Cord at the club the other night."

"So glad I could provide entertainment for their evening," she commented cynically.

"He hasn't been seen out with anyone since Britney died."

"Britney?" There was that name again. Maybe now she'd find out why it had been oddly familiar to her.

"Yeah, they were engaged. Last time anyone saw them together was the night he asked her to marry him at the club a little over two years ago, just before she went to the police academy."

"She was a cop?"

"Yup, Houston P.D. Died on her first patrol. Nearly destroyed Cord when the news came through she'd been shot."

Understanding dawned. "I remember that. I didn't work the case myself, but everyone assigned to it was focused on finding her killers."

"It was a bad time for everyone who knew Britney, but most of all for Cord. His parents even delayed their retirement to help him out."

"And he hasn't been out with anyone since?" she blurted without thinking.

The sheriff shook his head. "Folks wondered if you'd be staying on."

She barked a laugh. "No offense, Sheriff, but Royal's just a little too tame for me."

"That has its benefits," he said with a smile that showed he wasn't in the least offended.

Zoe held out her hand. "Thanks for everything. I'll be in touch."

"Thank you. And that file and the polygraph report will be waiting for you when you get to work tomorrow."

After shaking hands, she got into her car and tapped her address into the map app on her phone. Then with a final wave to the sheriff, she headed out of Royal.

As she drove, her mind began to wander. So Cord had been engaged, and she'd been his first relationship since then. Not that it made any difference. He'd gone out with her only to stop her from interviewing Jesse. She thought back to the day she'd met him, to his dismissive attitude of her being a cop. All the pieces fit. But none of it excused him for using her the way he had.

Eleven

Her eyes were grainy with exhaustion by the time she pulled into her parking garage, but at least she was home. She'd taken only a short break about two hours out of Houston to grab some food and something to drink at a gas station. *Food*, she snorted as she grabbed her bag and laptop. *Cardboard with processed meat and cheese, more like.* She wondered if there was anything edible left in her apartment. Unlikely, but she'd take her chances when she got upstairs.

She exited the elevator and turned down the corridor to her apartment. All weariness fled and adrenaline flooded her system as she spied someone loitering near her front door. She dropped her things and reached for her gun just as the man turned around to face her. Shock replaced the adrenaline as she identified Cord.

"What the hell are you doing here?" she demanded, holstering her gun and snatching up her things again.

"And how did you know where I live, let alone get past security?"

How dare he be here? And ahead of her, too. She'd driven the maximum speed limit the whole way here. Unless he'd been here waiting for her for all the hours it took to interview Stevens. She felt a perverse imp of satisfaction at the idea of him cooling his heels for several hours tweak her lips into a half smile.

"You're not the only one with investigative skills," Cord said with a grin that flashed across his features, then disappeared just as quickly. "I'm here to see you. We need to talk."

"No, we don't. We've done all the talking—all the anything—we needed to do."

"Seems we differ on that topic. Perhaps I should have said, *I* need to talk to you."

"And why should I listen to you? You willfully obstructed my investigation."

"I did."

"We have no more to say," she said adamantly and brushed past him to insert her key into the lock. "Enjoy your trip back to Royal."

"I'm not leaving until we've spoken."

"Then I hope you'll be comfortable sleeping out here on the hallway floor because I have nothing to say to you."

She went inside and started to close the door, but Cord swiftly blocked her action.

"Look, hear me out. Please? I know I was a prize asshole. I apologize for that."

"Good of you, but it makes no difference. I'm investigating a man's death here. You impeded that investigation."

"So arrest me."

They stared at each other in silence for a full minute. Zoe couldn't tear her gaze from his. She could see her own reflection in the darkness of his pupils, saw the determination in every line of his face. His lips, which could do such wicked things to her body, were compressed in a grim line, and the humor that she'd so often witnessed in his expression was not evident today. He wasn't going to leave until he'd said his piece, that much was blatantly clear. She blew out a sigh of frustration.

"Fine, come in. Five minutes and then you're out again. How the hell did you get here, anyway?"

"I flew in."

She stopped halfway through to the kitchen and dropped her bags onto a chair.

"Just like that?"

"The beauty of flying."

"No five-and-a-half-hour drive? No toilet stops in questionable bathrooms?"

He shook his head.

"I hate you," she muttered as she entered the kitchen and opened the refrigerator to stare blankly at its meager contents.

"Even more than this morning?" he said, stepping up close behind her and peering over her shoulder.

She felt his presence acutely, even though he wasn't touching her, and caught her breath so she wouldn't inhale the appealing scent of him. Whatever he smelled like, however good he felt against her body or even inside it, he'd betrayed her.

"Yes, even more than this morning."

"What if I head to the convenience store around the corner and get us some food and cook you dinner? Would you hate me less, then?"

She closed the fridge door with a thud and turned to face him. "No, I wouldn't. It's late, I'm tired, I'm frustrated and I want to go to sleep. Say what you wanted to say and go."

"Not even a coffee?"

She rolled her eyes and moved to the coffee machine. "Fine, and then you go."

She went through the motions, not even fully aware of what she was doing. All she could think about was Cord and the fact he was here, in her world now. Not that it made any difference. She'd closed that door. It wasn't even as if a future together had been in the cards in the first place. Friends with benefits, that was all it was. Heck, not even friends, to be totally blunt.

"I hope you like it black. Milk's off, and I don't have any powdered creamer," she said, pouring him a mug full of the dark brew.

"Thanks, it'll do fine."

He took the mug, his fingers brushing hers. She hated the cliché of it, but there was no mistaking the jolt of awareness she felt as their skin brushed.

"You're not having any?" he asked.

"No, I need to sleep. Gotta get into the station early."

"Right, so I guess my time starts now?"

Cord watched as Zoe nodded and gestured for him to sit in the living room. Before sitting down opposite him, she removed her holster and slid her weapon onto the table between them. A reminder, perhaps, that she was trained in firearms and not afraid to use them. Or simply just a reminder that she was and always would be a cop.

He drew in a deep breath and began to speak. "What I did was wrong."

"Y'think?" she answered caustically and arched one brow at him.

"Not just from a legal perspective, but from a personal one. I've never been the kind of person to cause trouble with the police."

"And yet you did."

She crossed her arms and stared at him. Nope—she definitely wasn't going to make this any easier.

"Look, initially, when I knew you were investigating Jesse, it sent me into protective mode. He's been through a lot."

"And you don't think the Hamm family has been through a lot, too? That they don't deserve some answers as to who murdered their son?"

He shook his head. "I was wrong. I knew Jesse couldn't have been involved. I just didn't want you hassling him. But—" he held up one hand as she started to interrupt "—I had no right to do what I did nor delay your opportunity to interview him. I apologize for all of it."

"Great, I accept your apology. You can go now."

She started to stand.

"Look, just a few more minutes," he begged. To his relief she sat back down again. "I'm fiercely attracted to you, Detective. It scares me."

"Go on."

"I was engaged before, to a girl named Britney Collins."

"I know the name."

"Then you know what happened to her."

"I do."

"I can't go through that again. I can't face every single day knowing a woman I love is putting herself in danger." *Love?* Where did that come from? He was messing this all up, especially if the suddenly shuttered look on Zoe's face was any indicator. "I was never keen on her career choice. In fact, I have to admit that I never fully understood her need or her drive to become one of Houston's finest. But I couldn't hold her back. If I'd asked her, she wouldn't have done it. Instead, she'd have found work in Royal that satisfied her until we had kids, and then she would have stayed home with them. But I knew she wanted more than that.

"Part of me regrets not being selfish. She'd still be alive today if I had. But, in time, she'd have been desperately unhappy. Which brings me to you."

Zoe's eyes widened slightly. "Look, what happened to Britney was awful. It's something every cop and their family dread, but you can't compare her situation to mine. I've been raised in a police family. I've been a cop for nine years. I'm not saying I won't ever get killed on the job, but I am saying I am well trained, and in my role as a detective, I'm not exposed to the kinds of things a frontline officer is on a daily basis.

"But, all of that said, I'm not in the market for a relationship. Especially not a long-distance one. Hell, I'd probably stand more chance of being involved in a car wreck than I do getting hurt on the job."

"Does that mean you're not even willing to try? We have a connection, Zoe. You know it. I know it. Don't you think it's worth exploring to see what happens?"

She shook her head slowly, and he could see regret in her eyes. "No. Your life, everything, is in Royal. Mine is here. We might fit in the bedroom, but we don't fit when it comes to our lifestyles or our careers.

"I know you have an obligation to your family, and that's what drives you on your ranch. It's your home, it's what you do and, from what I could see, you're good at it. It fits for you. This city, the people in it, that's what fits for me. We're oil and water, Cord. We just don't mix. I think you should go now."

He stood, even though every cell in his body was telling him to fight harder, to tell her he could change, make adjustments, that if they both wanted it enough, they could make it work. But deep down he knew it would be futile.

In fact, it would probably only lead to more heartbreak for both of them.

"Thanks for hearing me out," he said, offering Zoe his hand to shake when she'd walked him to the door.

She took his hand and squeezed it gently, but before she could let him go he tugged her slightly off balance, pulling her against him. Without a second thought he cupped her jaw, tilting her face up to his and taking her lips with a kiss that both seared her flesh and said a bittersweet goodbye.

He stood outside the door after she'd closed it. He wasn't giving up. She might think it was over between them, but he had to be 100 percent sure they couldn't make a go of this. Life was too short and way too precious not to fight for what was important. He knew that better than most. And he had an ace up his sleeve that Zoe wasn't expecting.

Cord started walking to the elevator. This round was hers, but he was pretty certain he'd win the next one.

Cord pulled up outside the sprawling home in a suburban part of Houston the next day. The lots were a generous size here, the gardens well established and there was an air of quiet gentility about the area, with echoes of past families having been raised around here. He checked the address he'd been given and looked at the house across the street. So this was where Zoe had grown up. He could just imagine a younger, skinnier version of her shinnying up one of those giant trees or riding her bike along the sidewalk.

He reached for the large colorful bunch of flowers on the passenger seat of his rental car and the bottle of red wine he'd bought and got out of the car. The older woman who opened the door to his knock was smiling widely.

"You must be Cord," she said. "Welcome to our home.

We're so grateful to you for looking out for Zoe while she was out of town."

"Mrs. Warren, lovely to meet you, and it was a pleasure. Can I just say how like Zoe you look, or should that be the other way around?"

"Ah yes, people do say that. Come on out back. The boys and their families are already here. We're just waiting for Zoe."

"These are for you," he said, giving Zoe's mom the bouquet of flowers.

"They're beautiful, thank you. You'll make my husband jealous," she said with a girlish giggle.

"Well, I have brought him a gift, too," Cord said, brandishing the bottle of wine. "So I hope he'll forgive me."

She spied the label. "Oh yes, he'll forgive you, all right. Follow me."

Cord trailed behind her, his eyes catching on a series of family photos that lined the hallway in groupings that appeared to be by various eras within the family. He'd have liked to have lingered and studied the progression of Zoe's childhood to the woman she was today, but Zoe's mom was disappearing through a doorway ahead of him. He quickly followed her through the door and was met by a cacophony of sound. Kids, dogs, family. It looked like there were people everywhere.

This was what Zoe had grown up surrounded by. It was very different from his upbringing as the only child of a close-knit ranching family. Sure, they'd had extended family to visit occasionally, and some of the hands lived on-site. And there had been the Stevens kids as well, but this was something else.

"Jed, come and meet Cord, the guy I was telling you about."

A heavyset grizzled man in his late fifties put down the

tongs he'd been using on the outdoor grill and wiped his hands on the apron he was wearing. The pink frilly fabric looked incongruous on him, but that fact didn't seem to bother him at all as he came over to meet Cord.

"Jed Warren. I'm Zoe's dad. Pleased to meet you."

"Cord Galicia. Likewise. This is for you," Cord said, handing the man the bottle of wine.

"Well, thank you very much. We invited you here to thank you for looking out for our girl, not for you to bring us stuff," Jed said with a grin.

"My mom always said I should never arrive anywhere empty-handed."

"Well, I appreciate this. I really do. In fact, I might just put this on the rack so it doesn't get quaffed by the riffraff here." Jed gestured toward four young men in the back-yard who, by their appearance, were obviously his sons.

Zoe's mom linked her arm in Cord's. "Come and meet the rest of the family, and please call me Sarah."

Cord made it through most of the introductions before completely losing track of which kids belonged to what parents, but there came a point when he felt a shift in the camaraderie of the moment to one of pointed observation. It coincided with an intense prickle of awareness running down his neck. Zoe was here. Slowly, he turned around and faced her. Fury and disbelief warred for dominance on her beautiful features.

Sarah Warren saw her daughter and bustled forward.

"Zoe, darling. Glad you could get away from work. Come, have a drink."

"What's he doing here?" she asked bluntly.

Cord saw color infuse her mother's cheeks. "Zoe," she whispered fiercely. "We don't treat our guests like that."

"He's a guest? Seriously? You invited him?"

"Of course we did. He called us, trying to track you

down. Said you'd left something at his house when he put you up after that dreadful motel fire. You remember, the one you didn't see fit to tell your mother about?"

Cord stifled a grin. There was nothing quite like a mother's love and censure all rolled into one telling off. Zoe, it seemed, felt the same way.

"Mom, it wasn't that bad. But I still don't understand why he's here."

"Well, when he called and asked for your address, we just wanted to say thank-you for his hospitality toward you, of course."

The way Sarah spoke, it made her invitation to him so very matter-of-fact, but he could see Zoe wasn't having any of it.

"Right," she said, in response to her mom's explanation. "Well, I can't stay long. I'm waiting for a call to get back to the office."

"Surely you can take a couple of hours away from your work," her mother admonished and grabbed an ice-cold beer from a fridge on the back porch and shoved it into her daughter's hand. "There, now have a drink and play nice."

Sarah went back inside the kitchen, leaving Cord and Zoe mostly alone on the back patio.

"Great place your parents have. Must have been fun growing up here."

"With that lot?" she gestured with her beer bottle to her brothers, who'd lined up on either side of a picnic table to have a drink and a yarn while their wives supervised the children for a while. "Hardly."

"I bet it was fun," Cord said again, this time with a wistfulness to his voice that he hadn't expected.

"Are you stalking me?" Zoe said after a short silence.

"What? No!"

"It certainly looks that way."

"Look, I called your parents' house after you left because you left your computer cable behind. I wanted to know where I could send it. I explained to your mom why you'd been staying with me, and she gave me your address and then when I said I'd be in Houston, she invited me for dinner tonight. I could hardly refuse."

"Oh yes, you could totally have refused." Zoe took a swig of her beer and turned to face him. "And you still haven't given me my computer cable."

"Let's just say I got distracted yesterday. It's in my car now. I was going to leave it with your parents if you didn't show."

"You mean you didn't think I'd be here tonight?"

"Your mom wasn't sure if you'd make it. Seems you don't make it to a lot of family get-togethers these days."

Zoe groaned. "Don't you start. I get enough of that from Mom."

Cord shrugged. "Only repeating what she told me."

He looked at her. There were dark shadows under her eyes, giving them a bruised look and making her look more vulnerable than he'd ever seen her. He couldn't help himself. He reached out to touch her cheek. A slight buzz tingled through his fingertips as they grazed gently against her skin.

"You okay? You look tired."

She shook her head, breaking the contact. "I'm fine. This investigation is driving me insane, though. There's a whole ton of pressure from the top brass to wrap this up, like, you have no idea."

"And I made that worse for you, didn't I? I'm truly sorry. I wasn't thinking."

"Look, I accepted your apology," she said testily and took another sip of her beer.

"I know, but I meant it. Look, I won't stay. I can see that my being here is spoiling it for you."

Cord put his beer down on the table next to them and started to walk away. He was surprised when Zoe grabbed his arm.

"Don't you dare leave. It'll be more than my life is worth trying to explain it after you've gone."

He stopped and looked at her. She was glancing between him and her brothers, all of whom had turned to watch them with varying degrees of interest.

"Okay," he said and picked up his beer again. "Again, my apologies—this wasn't a good idea."

"No, it wasn't, but you're here now, so let's make the most of it. I take it you've met everybody?"

"Yeah. I like your family so far."

She snorted. "Well, the fact that you're still alive probably means they like you, too. Either that or they've decided you're an experiment."

"How so?"

"They're probably taking bets to see how long it'll take me to screw this up."

He raised his brows at her. "You do that often?"

She punched him in the arm. "I get enough cheek from that bunch over there," she said, nodding in the direction of her brothers. "If you're staying, you're my ally, okay?"

He shrugged. "Sure. Does that mean I get to kiss you again?"

In an instant the atmosphere between them thickened and changed into something far more intense. The sounds of the kids playing in the yard, of Jed grilling the meat and Sarah calling her boys to help bring salads out from the house all faded into the background. All Cord could focus on was Zoe's mouth. On the way her lips glistened with a sheen of moisture on the remnants of the lipstick she must have applied a while ago but that had mostly worn away. He wanted to remove the rest of it—with a scrape of his teeth, a rasp of his tongue, with the pressure of his lips.

Heat poured through his body and arousal followed swiftly after. He continued to stare at Zoe, and she remained silent in response. Her eyes had widened slightly, her pupils almost consuming the blue irises that told so much and yet hid so much at the same time. Cord realized that while he knew exactly how to bring her to a screaming climax, he knew very little about Zoe Warren, the woman. And he wanted to. Oh, how he wanted to. What had started as a distraction had wormed its way deep into his psyche and gone way beyond the physical attraction that sparked like fallen power lines between them.

This was so much more, and it was equally as dangerous at the same time.

Twelve

Zoe's breath caught in her chest. One minute they'd been bantering, she on the point of asking him to leave, until he'd gone and offered to do so—and she'd realized that she didn't want him to go after all. In fact, he was the reason she looked so darn tired today. It had nothing to do with the early start back at the station and everything to do with cursing herself for making him leave last night.

The truth was he frightened her. He was intense about everything he did—from seeing to his ranch to stroking her body to flaming life. She couldn't handle it. Didn't want to. And did, all at the same time. Cord Galicia had turned her on her head and she didn't like it one bit. Worse, he was distracting her from her work even when he wasn't deliberately trying to hold her back from doing her job. He'd inveigled his way into every crevice in her mind, meaning thoughts of him—reminders of his scent, the way he moved, the way he tasted—would unexpectedly send ripples of desire through her body at the most inopportune moments.

Last night, after she'd closed the door on him and sent him away—for good, she'd believed—she ended up going to her room and collapsing onto her bed, clutching her pillow to her body like some lovelorn teenager. She wasn't that person, and yet, somehow, he'd made her like that. Made her want him. Worse, he'd made her need him. She'd been unable to sleep in anything more than short snatches, and she'd been short-tempered with her team when she'd gone into the station this morning and they'd ribbed her about her vacation in the country.

There'd been no further progress on her case. She'd reviewed the sound and video files and polygraph results sent through from Sheriff Battle's office, looking for a loophole she might have missed, but they merely confirmed Jesse Stevens was totally clean. She'd even had his alibi checked out, although his receipts had been conclusive in themselves.

And then there was Cord.

She realized that her family was beginning to give them strange looks, as if they'd both missed something going on around them. And they had. While she and Cord had been locked in their bubble, the world had continued around them.

"Aunty Zoe, are you in love?"

The piercingly innocent curiosity of one of her nieces shook her from the spell she'd fallen under.

"What makes you say that, Theresa?" she asked, bending down to the four-year-old's level.

"'Cause you're looking at that man like mommy looks at daddy when she says she wants to eat him all up." Theresa took a deep breath. "And mommy loves daddy."

"Out of the mouths of babes," Cord murmured from behind her.

"Don't encourage her," Zoe said over her shoulder before smiling at her little niece. She rose, taking the little girl's hand. "No, honey. I'm not in love. But I am hungry for dinner. Are you?"

The rest of the evening passed relatively uneventfully. To her relief, Cord gave her some distance and didn't stick to her side. Even so, she was constantly physically aware of his every move. Even the way he tipped his beer to his lips sent a pull of longing through her. By the time her brothers and their wives started to gather up their kids and head home, it was getting late and exhaustion dragged at her.

Cord had been busy in the kitchen, helping clean up, when she decided it was time for her to go. Her mom, bless her heart, shooed Cord from the kitchen, telling him she and Jed could manage just fine from here. As a result, Zoe and Cord walked out together, and instead of her parents standing on the front porch and waving at her until she was out of sight, she had to fight back a tug of humor at her lips when her mom grabbed her dad by his arm and dragged him back inside immediately and shut the front door with a bang.

"Nice touch with the flowers for my mom, Galicia," Zoe said as she walked to her car with Cord shadowing at her side.

"I like to pay my respects. You have a nice family."

"Yeah, as much as I like to complain about them, I love them dearly. I couldn't stand to be too far away. It's not often we can all get together at the same time. We're all on different shift rosters, so whenever there's a free Sunday, Mom puts on an evening like this."

"Family is important."

"It's one of the reasons I'll never leave Houston," Zoe said firmly.

She needed to make it clear that she'd meant what she said back in Royal. No matter how powerful this attraction between them, there was no way it could ever work. Her job aside, she'd slowly die inside if she was that far from the network of her parents and siblings.

"I understand," Cord said quietly, his hands shoved into his jeans pockets as if he had to confine them to stop himself from reaching for her.

A part of her wished he would. Wished he'd take her into his arms and kiss her, right here on the street in full view of anyone. Instead, he tugged his keys out of his pocket.

"Good night, Zoe. It's been great. But I get the message. I'd hoped we could figure it out—make us work somehow—but now, having seen your family and you with them, I truly do understand what keeps you here. It's not just your job, because I know you'd be a great cop anywhere, and it's not the city. It's them, and you don't need to make any apology for that. Family is the glue that holds us together."

"Well, they're a pain in the butt most of the time, but yeah."

"They only want you to be happy. To have what they have."

Unexpected tears sprang to Zoe's eyes. His words cut her to her soul. She wanted that, too, but she wanted to be so much more than that at the same time. Somehow she'd just never envisaged being able to juggle it all. Her job had defined her for nine years, and, yes, she'd put her work ahead of everything and everyone she'd met along the way. With her dad and brothers being in the force, it had made it easier for her to hone her focus, even though they'd always teased her about settling down one day. But, at the same time, they balanced their work and family life without any serious problems.

But it would be different with Cord if they ever did try to make things work between them. He'd already lost a woman he'd loved to her job and in the worst way possible. Zoe had pulled the incident report and skimmed it when she'd gotten into work today. The facts had been chilling. No wonder Cord was so put off by guns and the people who carried them in their line of work.

He was walking away now, and she felt as if she was being torn in two. One half of her urging her to let him go, the other begging her to make him stay, even if only for one more night. The flip side won.

"Cord!"

She was moving toward him before she even realized it. The moment he turned, she reached for him, tugging his face down to hers. She kissed him—hard and fierce and with every ounce of longing that pulsed through her body.

"Come back to my place, please?"

He stared at her a full twenty seconds before replying. She could see the battle that raged behind his beautiful sherry-brown eyes. He closed them a moment, his long lashes sweeping down. They should look ridiculous on a man like him, a man who was so lean and fierce and strong, but instead they only made him look that much more appealing.

"Yes."

It was one simple word, just three letters, and yet it had the power to make her feel as if she'd won the lottery ten times over.

"Follow me," she said and all but ran back to her car.

He tailed her the few short miles back to her apartment building, pulling into the visitor parking he'd used the day before while she put her car in the parking garage. She ran up the ramp to where he was waiting at the front of the building, and she grabbed his hand and tugged him through the front door. She barely acknowledged security when they greeted her; she had only one thought burning through her mind. If this was to be their last time together, it had to be perfect, because it would have to last her forever.

The ride in the elevator was interminable, but finally they spilled out of the car and down the hallway to her apartment. She just managed to wrestle her door open and tumble inside her apartment with Cord right behind her. She grabbed him by his shoulders and pushed him up against the wall the second the door was closed and secured behind them. She tugged at his jacket, then his shirt, exposing the warm, tanned skin of his chest to her gaze, her fingers, her mouth.

He groaned and tangled his fingers in her hair as she kissed him and dragged her lips down his throat, nipping at the cords of his neck, then soothing them with her tongue. Her hands were busy at his belt, unbuckling it and then unbuttoning his fly with a dexterity that amazed her under the conditions. She shoved his jeans down his lean hips and her hand cupped his engorged shaft through his boxer briefs.

Cord didn't waste any time. He tugged at the buttons of her blouse and opened her jeans with equal alacrity, and she toed off her ankle boots and stepped out of her jeans, standing now on legs that trembled. His heated palm cupped her between her legs, and she just about went ballistic on the sensation of heat, silk and moisture against her most sensitive skin.

And then he was lifting her up against him. She hooked her legs around him and held on tight.

"Bedroom?"

"First door on the right past the sitting room," she directed.

He walked them both to the bedroom and dropped her unceremoniously onto the bed, but the second he joined her on the mattress she straddled him again, smoothing her hands in hurried caresses over his shoulders, his chest, his belly.

"You feel so good," she murmured and bent down to kiss him, her tongue teasing his, her teeth nipping gently at his lower lip, tugging it before swiping it with her tongue and kissing him hard.

Her entire body hummed for this man, and she couldn't wait to feel him inside her, stroking her to another amazing crescendo of feeling and sensation, but she could prolong the agony of waiting just a little longer if she could feast her eyes on him and touch him in all the places she longed to. Zoe traced the lean lines of muscle that defined his stomach, letting her fingers edge ever closer to the waistband of his briefs. She skimmed the elastic, then started from the top of his shoulders all over again.

"Detective, is there anything in particular you're looking for? Because you seem to be examining my body of evidence rather thoroughly."

She chuckled and nipped him in the hollow just inside his hip bone. He laughed in response.

"Don't rush me," she growled and pinched the side of his leg in punishment.

"Wouldn't dream of it," he replied.

Cord bunched his fists in her bedcovers and lifted his hips slightly as she slid her fingers beneath his waistband and began tugging his briefs off. His erection sprang proudly free of its confines, and Zoe smiled as she anticipated what she would do next.

"Seriously, Detective? You're just going to look at it?"

Stifling another chuckle, she looked up at his face

and gave him a stern stare. "Like I said, Galicia, don't rush me."

"Or what?"

"Or you might live to regret it."

"Are you going to torture me? I could get used to that."

She ignored the pang his words engendered. Get used to it? Get used to her? That wouldn't happen. She'd made it clear outside her parents' place. And then she'd muddied the waters by inviting him back here.

"Zoe?"

She looked into his eyes, saw the concern there.

"Just dreaming up a suitable punishment," she answered lightly.

She turned her attention to Cord's very enticing body and in particular to one very demanding shaft of flesh. She closed her fingers around the hot, hard rod and stroked him from base to tip before taking him into her mouth. He groaned again, and she teased him with her tongue and her lips until she knew he was almost at the point of no return. She released him from the warm, wet confines of her mouth and blew softly against his skin.

"Detective, I think you need to take me into custody soon or I might not be responsible for my actions."

"Duly noted," she said with a smile as she stretched over him and reached for the bedside cabinet drawer.

She grabbed a handful of condoms and dropped them onto the bed beside them before selecting one and smoothing it onto his straining flesh. Then, without wasting another moment, she straddled him again and guided him into her body, slowly and deliberately taking him inside her inch by slow inch. The expression on his face was one of pure concentration and control, as if he could slip at any moment. She loved the idea that she did this to him and that he let her.

Zoe rocked her hips, taking him that little deeper, clenching against his hardness, then releasing him, setting up a rhythm that increased in tempo until she could control herself no longer. And then she was lost on that wave of pure bliss, her internal muscles spasming and pulling Cord right along with her on that journey to the stars and back again. She collapsed over him, her body slick with perspiration and every nerve shuddering with the power of her climax. Inside her, she could feel him swell and twitch as the last of his orgasm pulsed into satiation and, finally, calm.

Cord's arms wrapped around her and he rolled them onto their sides, and together they slid into sleep, only to wake two hours later and take each other all over again. This time it was Cord who led the way, tormenting her to a point where she felt as though she might shatter into a thousand pieces, before taking her to even greater heights of pleasure.

When Zoe woke in the morning, it was to an empty bed and an empty apartment—and an even emptier heart. She sank onto the sofa in her living room, wrapped in one of her bedsheets, and bent her head and cried for all that they'd shared together and all that they would never have again. She knew now that it went beyond sex. Way beyond it. Somewhere along the line he'd stolen her heart. But it was a love that could never work, she reminded herself. She wouldn't compromise on that which was most important to her. Her family. Her work. And he knew that. Accepted it. Because he'd left without a goodbye, and now it was up to her to deal with that.

Eighteen-year-old Maya Currin synced her playlist to her car and settled in for the drive. The baby of Ryder Currin's kids, she knew if she'd told her family she was coming home, someone would have flown to drive her down or at least accompany her on the long journey from Boston back to Texas. But she didn't want company because she had plenty of thinking to do along the way. Not the least of which was clearing her head of that waste of space she'd called her boyfriend.

How could she have been so stupid to have thought Dirk had truly loved her? All he'd loved was her last name and the kudos that came with being one of the children of the famed oil baron and businessman, Ryder Currin. But she wasn't a real Currin, was she? No, she'd been adopted, and apparently discovering that had been enough for her boyfriend to stop pretending to love her anymore.

She shook her head as she put her car on cruise control after entering the I-81. How could she have been so stupid, so gullible? It was the latter that irked her the most. Her dad had always told her that people would like her for their position, for their money. She hadn't believed him and, believing she was a good judge of character, had delighted in proving him wrong. When she met Dirk, she truly believed every word that fell from his lying lips. Well, more fool her. Her love affair with him, however intense and brief, had momentarily distracted her from her quest to find out the truth about her birth. She'd always known her father knew far more than he'd ever let on, and she'd stopped worrying about it when she'd fallen in love.

But no more. Now she was going to get to the bottom of it. To find out what her birth story really was. She deserved to know. She was an adult, after all. Her father had promised he'd tell her the truth once she was eighteen and he owed her that truth now.

Being rejected for not being a real Currin was one thing. She could get over that and the idiot who'd even had the nerve to say such a stupid thing. But suffering the perpetual sense of disconnection from her father and her older siblings, Xander and Annabel—that was something else.

Yes, she'd known and accepted that Ryder Currin had cho-sen to raise her with Annabel's mom, Elinah. Elinah, Ry-der's second wife, had, until her death when Maya was only five, been the only mother figure Maya had known. As a kid, she'd never questioned why they'd adopted her and brought her up as their own. Her adoption had been private and closed—which had sent up some flags when she'd tried to investigate exactly who her birth parents were. She had a right to know. A right to her history.

Every time she had a question it seemed as though there was yet another secret barring her from knowing the truth. Her father had told her over and over that the truth had no bearing on their relationship, that he loved her and that was all that mattered. But how could she continue to be-lieve him and trust in his love for her when he wouldn't tell her who she really was?

The thought of walking away from the only family she'd ever known sliced through her like a physical pain. It was almost unthinkable, but if she didn't find the answers she sought, she didn't know if she could continue to pretend to be a part of them all. She needed to know the truth, and her father was the only person who could give that to her.

She'd decided this was important enough now to give up a week or more of her classes. Maybe she'd even take a break for the rest of this semester and return to Boston College again in the winter—with the truth in hand and her place in the world all the more secure.

Maya changed lanes and passed a long rig before easing back into the right-hand lane again. While she was eager to find answers, she wasn't exactly in a mad hurry for this confrontation. After all, she'd waited her lifetime to hear what her father would have to say, if he'd even say it, and she wanted to arrive safely and in one piece.

Thirteen

Cord kicked off his boots in the mudroom and walked into the house, heading immediately to the kitchen refrigerator. He snagged a beer by its neck and strolled back outdoors into the loggia. Damn, even here he couldn't rid himself of memories of Zoe.

The entire past week he'd been working every hour he could, even going so far as to repaint the sheds. Anything to keep busy and keep his mind off that woman. Thing was, nothing was working. No matter how tired he made himself, she'd inveigle her way into his thoughts.

He threw himself onto one of the outdoor sofas and leaned back to take a long pull of his beer. He grimaced as he swallowed it. Even that didn't taste any good. A sound from inside the house drew his attention, putting all his senses on alert. He wasn't expecting anyone, and thieves didn't usually bother this far out of town. He put his beer down on the table and rose to his feet, carefully opening the kitchen door and moving swiftly and silently through the lower floor.

He heard a sound again. This time there was no mistaking it. It came from the suite of rooms his grandmother had used. He doubted she'd left her valuables behind after the move to Palm Springs, but, either way, he hated the thought of someone pawing through her stuff. He reached for a tall brass candlestick off the hallway table and gripped it firmly in one hand as he carefully pushed the door open.

"Argh!" his grandmother screamed, and she dropped the clothes she'd been lifting from her suitcase on the bed.

She broke into a voluble stream of Spanish, telling her grandson in no uncertain terms precisely how many years he'd just shaved off her life. Cord threw the candlestick onto the bed and stepped forward to grab his grandmother and hug her tight. She was so tiny she barely even reached his chin, but her strong arms folded around his waist, just the way they had always done, and he felt her begin to calm down.

"What are you doing here?" he asked, still stunned to have discovered she was his intruder.

"Bah, Palm Springs. It's not for me," she said, tugging herself loose and bending to pick up the scattered clothing. "Maybe it's nice for a holiday, but I can't live like that. There's nothing to do!"

"Isn't that the point of being retired?" Cord said as he picked up a stray pair of his grandmother's voluminous underwear and passed them to her.

She snatched them from him with a sniff of disdain. "Retired? That was your father's idea. Not mine. He's my son and I love him but…" She shook her head vehemently. "Palm Springs is slowly driving him loco. I don't know how your mother stands it."

"But wasn't Palm Springs her idea?"

His grandmother made a dismissive snort. "Only after your father started talking about it. You know how he always needs to be led. Oh, he's a hard worker, but he has to be allowed to think things are his idea. When he talked about Palm Springs and retiring, I don't think either of them had the slightest idea of what it meant. Sure, they've made new friends, but it's not—what is it you people say? Their scene?"

Cord sat on the bed and watched as Abuelita moved around the room, putting her things away.

"Anyway," she continued, "I've had enough of being retired. So I came back to take care of you."

"I'm a grown man, Abuelita. I can take care of myself," Cord pointed out with a rueful grin.

His grandmother settled onto the comforter beside him. She raised a gnarled hand to his face, cupping his cheek and forcing him to look deep into her eyes.

"If that is so, my boy, then why do you carry so much pain in your eyes? Is it a woman? Let me talk to her. I'll fix it for you."

Cord laughed, the first genuine joy he'd felt since he'd slipped from Zoe's bed and disappeared into the early strains of morning. The thought of Abuelita fronting up to Zoe and giving her a piece of her mind would be worth the price of ringside seats, for sure, but this was his problem and since it couldn't be dealt with, it would simply have to be left to fade away.

"I see all your easy living hasn't softened your edges," he teased her, bending down to kiss the top of her head.

"Don't try to distract me, Cord. I know when something isn't right here." She pressed a fist to her chest. "Tell me."

"Talking about it won't fix things," he said firmly. "We're too different. We knew it wouldn't work from the start."

"But you still got burned, yes?"

He nodded.

"It's good that you were prepared to open your heart again. I was scared that when you lost Britney, you would never trust yourself to love another woman." She sighed and patted his cheek before taking his hand. "Tell your *abuelita* about this woman. Tell me everything."

"She's a cop," he said on a deep sigh and felt his grandmother's fingers tighten almost painfully around his own.

"Go on," she prompted.

He told her the story of how they'd met. How unhelpful he'd been, how he'd deliberately distracted her from being able to meet with Jesse.

"And she still agreed to see you? Is the girl mad? I would have run a mile from you."

"As I remember, you did run several miles from Abuelo. Didn't he have to come and fetch you to the church on the day of your wedding because you said you'd changed your mind?"

"Pah!" She waved a hand contemptuously. "I needed to be certain he loved me, that is all."

"And he did."

Her face softened on a memory. "Yes, he did. But he would have been ashamed of what you have done to this girl. What did you call her? Zoo-ee?"

"Zoe," he corrected her. "And I was pretty ashamed of myself, too."

"So did you not apologize?"

"I did."

"And she didn't accept it?"

"She did."

"Then I don't understand. What is wrong?"

"She lives in Houston. Her whole life is there. Her family, her career. Everything that is important to her."

"Are you not important to her, too? You young people

today. You want it all your own way. You don't understand compromise. I did not want to leave Mexico, my family, my whole life, to come here to Texas. But your grandfather had a dream, and as his wife it was my role to support him in that dream."

"I know, Abuelita, and he loved you all the more for that. But I don't see how Zoe and I can work this out. I went to her, but she made it very clear that her life is in Houston. She won't budge on that. And I can't leave all this. You and Abuelo built it up for Dad and for me and future generations of Galicias. I can't just walk away. I have a responsibility to our name and to the land."

His grandmother was silently shaking her head. "Your *abuelo* never wanted this to be your prison, my boy."

"It's not a prison. I love my home. I love what it means to our whole family. I'm honored that it now falls to me to look after the legacy."

He said the words with vehemence, but the passion behind them was no longer in his heart.

"That might have been true before your Zoo-ee," his grandmother said with her usual uncanny insightfulness. "But it is not true anymore. I can see why you are unhappy."

"I'm not unhappy," he protested automatically, but even as he did so, he felt the sharp sting of regret pierce his heart. Regret for what might have been had the circumstances been completely different.

But then again, if circumstances were different, wouldn't he and Zoe be different people, too? Would they have come together as hastily as they had? Experienced the heights they'd shared? For all that they had no future together, he couldn't regret a moment of the time they'd had.

Cord had spent a lot of time thinking since Abuelita's return a couple of days ago. And he'd come to a decision.

After his grandmother had gone to bed, he lifted the phone and called his parents.

The sound of his father's voice as he picked up the phone in Palm Springs was instantly calming in the way that only a parent could soothe a child, no matter their age.

"Dad, we need to talk," Cord said after the obligatory greetings had been dealt with.

"This sounds serious. Should I sit down?"

"I can hear the bedsheets, Dad. I know you're lying down already," Cord said with a grin.

"What's up, son?"

"I think you and mom should come back. Take charge of the ranch again. No, hear me out," Cord interjected as his father started to object. "It's not that I can't manage, but I think you left too early. Tell me you're not bored stupid at the end of every day. Tell me you don't miss the herd, the land, the work."

"I don't miss getting up at dawn every damn day," his father grumbled.

"So you start your days a little later. But, Dad, come home where you belong."

"Did Abuelita put you up to this?" Cord's father demanded.

"No, not at all. It's been on my mind awhile. You know I've been diversifying the herd, raising goats, making goat cheese. I want to expand that side of the business, and I can't do it on my own, especially if I'm managing the beef herds and breeding program, too. I need you to come back and work the ranch again. Obviously the choice is yours, but there's a business opportunity that's opened up for me closer to Houston. To make it work, I need you here. If you're certain you don't want to come back, I'll let that opportunity go, because I could never leave this place without ensuring a Galicia is at the head of operations. I respect my heritage too much to do that. What do you think?"

Cord held his breath as he waited for his father's response. His dad's voice was choked with emotion when he spoke.

"I have a good many years left in me, and, yes, while I like the idea of calling my time my own and doing what I want when I want, it took coming here to make me realize that what I want most is whatever's happening on the ranch. But I made my choice, son. I walked away. The ranch is yours now."

Cord gripped the phone so tight he thought he might break it. He forced his hand to relax.

"Dad, walk back. *Mi casa es su casa*, you know that. I never wanted you to go in the first place. When can you get here? Tomorrow?" He laughed, feeling as though a massive weight had been lifted from his shoulders.

"Not quite so fast. We have some things to wrap up here, sell the apartment, pack. Maybe the day after tomorrow," his father joked. In the background, Cord could hear his mother's excited voice. "Your mother is looking forward to seeing you, too, by the way."

"I've missed you guys. We have a lot to talk about when you get back. You see, I've met a girl."

"A girl? What's she li—"

In an instant Cord's mother was on the phone.

"You've met a girl? What's she like? Tell me everything. Well, not everything. But tell me about her."

Cord fought back a smile. No, he would definitely not be telling his mother everything, but he knew it wouldn't hurt to have his mother's perspective on what he planned to do. His feelings for Zoe were too deep for him to take any risks. This had to be perfect, and getting his family on board with the idea was only the first rung on the ladder.

Fourteen

"Flowers for you, Detective," one of Zoe's colleagues announced as he brought a large colorful display of blooms to her desk. "Have to say, they brighten things up around here. Maybe they can lift some of that sour expression you've been wearing these past two weeks."

"My expression is none of your business," Zoe snapped. "Aren't there some follow-up interviews you're supposed to be doing?"

Her fellow detective snapped to attention and executed a sharp salute. "Yes, ma'am. Right on it, ma'am."

She heard him laughing as he left the squad room and fought back a smile of her own. He was a damn fine detective, but he also knew exactly which buttons to push to get her ruffled. You'd think after nine years on the force she'd have developed a tougher hide for this kind of thing, but all it took was something that essentially reminded her she was female to make her even more hard-assed than ever before.

Sour? Really? She was just doing her job. The scent of the flowers tickled her nose and reminded her of what had triggered her current less-than-wonderful mood in the first place. Flowers? Seriously, who sent flowers these days? And why to her work? It wasn't her birthday or any special anniversary of anything. She eyed the arrangement as if it hid a venomous snake somewhere in the cheerful collection of buds and blossoms and spied the envelope that was buried in their midst.

She yanked the envelope out and flicked open the flap, which already bore evidence of having been opened and read by at least one of her colleagues before being brought to her desk. She groaned. She'd never hear the end of this.

I miss you.

The message was short, sweet and unsigned. She felt a flush of heat tinge her cheeks as she read the three words again. There was only one person who could have sent these to her. Cord Galicia. Well, she'd give him a piece of her mind. She snatched her phone off the desk and started to punch in his number before realizing that she actually knew it by heart. What did that say about her?

Slowly, she put her phone back onto her desk, then rose to her feet and grabbed the flowers and walked out to where the captain's personal assistant was sitting.

"Here, Josie," she said, leaving them on the older woman's desk. "These are for you. A mark of appreciation for all you do for us."

The woman eyed them carefully before looking up at Zoe. "Weren't these the flowers that just arrived for you?"

Zoe shrugged. "Busted. But they're no good for my allergies. Would you like them or should I just toss them?"

Josie looked horrified at the very thought. "You will do no such thing. I'll drop them at my mother's care center on the way home. They love a splash of color in their main living room. At least they'll be appreciated there."

Zoe didn't miss the censure in Josie's voice. It was clear the woman didn't believe her excuse about allergies and felt she ought to be grateful someone had sent her such an extravagance, but Zoe didn't do guilt. Life was way too short.

Even so, as she walked back to her desk and shredded the note into confetti before putting the pieces into her trash bin, she couldn't help but cast her eye back at Josie's desk for one last look at the flowers.

The flowers were only the beginning. Over the next few days it seemed that Cord had begun a seduction on her, sending small gifts with a thoughtful message each time. A part of her loved them. Who wouldn't love the sinfully expensive body lotion he'd sent, which paired with her favorite perfume so perfectly, she argued against the inner voice that told her to throw it away. And the small basket of gourmet goodies had been highly appreciated in the squad room at morning break yesterday. In fact, her team was beginning to look forward to the daily deliveries with more anticipation than she did.

But the parcel that arrived today had been the last straw. Despite her best intentions to keep secret the sinfully seductive sapphire-blue silk underwear he'd sent her, the lacy bra and matching thong had slid from their wrapper and onto her desk before she could hide them.

The catcalls and hoots of laughter brought even the captain from his office to see what the fuss was. By then, Zoe had scrunched the pieces into the tissue and summarily dispatched them into her trash bin. Regrettably, the note with the words *I would give anything to see you in these* had been snatched from her hands and circulated around the squad room before she could grab it back.

At this rate she'd never be taken seriously at work again. It had to stop, and very soon she'd make that call to Cord that she'd been putting off. Tonight, she told herself. As soon as she'd followed up with the crime-scene techs on a piece of evidence they'd finally been able to get to that had been extracted from the Hamm murder scene.

She let herself into the lab and went straight to Kane, the tech who'd asked her to come.

"What is it?" Zoe said, coming straight to the point. "Tell me it's good news."

"Well, there's some good news. We're finally working through the last of the evidence that was collected at the murder scene. Obviously you know the scene was severely compromised by the flood—"

"Kane, don't waste my time by telling me what I already know. I need something to go on."

"Well, there's this."

Kane turned his computer screen toward her and magnified the picture displayed there. "As you can see, it's a human hair."

"You've examined plenty of human hair found at the crime scene. What makes this any different?"

"Well, it's not like the others in that it's naturally wavy and, get this, naturally red."

"So we're looking for someone with long, naturally wavy red hair?"

"Very possibly. Now, of course you know we can't determine sex from a single hair, unless—"

"Unless there is a root attached. Tell me there's a root attached."

Kane's face lit up. "Yup. This is definitely from a woman. Obviously we can't determine age, but we can narrow it down to an adult versus a child."

"Did you run the DNA? Did we get any hits in the system? A name, anything?" she demanded, trying her level best not to get excited at the news.

She hoped this could potentially lead her to Hamm's killer, because goodness only knew everything else at the scene had driven them from one dead end to another.

"Not yet. We only just uncovered this information in the last few hours. I thought you'd appreciate knowing straightaway."

"I do. I definitely do. Thanks, Kane. Let me know the minute you have anything else."

"Will do."

Zoe was almost in a good mood as she reentered the squad room, right up until the moment she saw the lingerie she'd thrown into the trash displayed on a crime-scene board behind her desk, with the heading Wanted... by Someone. A slow-burning rage filled her, but she knew better than to let any of that show to her team. She wouldn't give them the pleasure, but she'd sure as heck give Cord Galicia what was coming to him the second she got home tonight. She planned on leaving his ears so blistered he wouldn't bother her ever again. She pulled the lingerie off the board and furiously scored out the heading, then settled at her desk, acting as if nothing of importance was going on. Eventually, this would all settle down. It had to, because there was no future for her and Cord.

"Stop stalking me."

The smile that had been on Cord's face when he'd seen Zoe's caller ID on his phone began to fade. She sounded really pissed.

"I'm merely expressing my affection," he responded, fighting to keep his voice level.

There was one thing about this woman—she could get him from cold to burning hot in about three seconds flat.

The fact that this time the heat had everything to do with irritation and nothing to do with sexual attraction was neither here nor there. No one had ever had the ability to excite or incite him so effectively.

"Well, stop it. It's gone far enough. I thought I made myself clear when I said we have no future."

"You did," he agreed and leaned back against the fence railing behind him.

It was getting dark, and he probably should head inside soon but he enjoyed the peace of the late evening. Would enjoy it even better if he had someone special to share it with.

"Then why do you keep sending me stuff?"

"Tokens."

"What?"

"They're not stuff. They're tokens of my—" He paused for a moment before he said something he'd really rather say face-to-face and not over a phone connection.

"I don't care what they are, and I don't want them. Cord, really, this has to stop. You're making me a laughingstock at work."

Ah, and there it was. There was genuine pain behind her words. It wasn't the gifts she was objecting to—well, maybe not completely—it was where he was sending them. He hadn't thought through the ribbing she'd be getting at work. He'd seen them in a display in town and couldn't think past the mental picture of seeing her on his big, wide bed wearing them.

"You want me to send them to your apartment?" he offered, knowing exactly what the response would be.

She didn't disappoint. For the next several minutes, Cord held his phone away from his ear while Zoe went on a tirade that showed a far more inventive use of expletives and instructions of where to put certain things in a person's anatomy than he'd ever heard before. He was seriously impressed, although there was pretty much nothing about Zoe Warren that didn't impress him. When she finally settled into silence, he put the phone back to his ear.

"I'm sorry. It wasn't my intention to distress you, Detective."

"I'm not distressed," she snapped back. "I'm angry. You're not respecting my wishes. I don't want to see you anymore."

He felt the words like each one was an individual blow straight to his chest.

"But you don't hate me, right?" He couldn't resist digging at her one more time.

Her growl of frustration filled his ear until it was abruptly cut off as she severed the call. He nodded to himself. Yeah, she didn't hate him. She was just driven to do her job to the best of her ability, and she didn't see how she could make time for anyone, let alone him. Well, it was up to him to show her he could fit in her world, and maybe, just maybe, she'd change her mind.

It took a lot less time than he anticipated to get all his plans in motion. Turned out his parents had little emotional attachment to the things they had in their Palm Springs apartment and were happy to leave the place staged with all their new appliances and furniture and leave everything in the hands of the real estate agents. They'd arrived back home a week after his phone call, tired after the road trip but joyful to be back. And he welcomed them with open arms. Abuelita couldn't be more in her element with all her family under one roof again, and Cord wondered how she'd take the news of what he planned to do. To his surprise she'd merely nodded, patted him on the cheek and told him that a man needed to do what a man needed to do.

So now it was a matter of convincing the woman of his heart that she needed him, too. How hard could that be? Cord grimaced as he readied the helicopter for the flight to Houston, in no doubt this would likely be the most difficult thing he'd ever done. He stowed the package he'd painstakingly wrapped for her, one last gift in an attempt to win her heart, and towed the chopper from the hangar.

"You're really doing this, then?" a voice asked him from behind.

Cord turned around and smiled at Jesse. "Damned if I don't."

His best friend raised his brows in surprise. "Seems all rather sudden, don't you think?"

"When you know, you know," Cord said. "And I know if I don't try this one last time, I'll regret it for the rest of my life."

Jesse stepped forward with his hand outstretched. "Then I can only wish you the best, buddy."

Cord clasped his best friend's hand firmly. "Thanks. I need all the help I can get."

He climbed aboard and fired up the chopper as Jesse took the ground-handling wheels back inside the hangar for him. In a matter of minutes he was skyward and headed toward Houston with hope and trepidation warring for dominance deep inside him.

Cord hangared the chopper just outside Houston, the way he'd done on his last visit, and picked up his rental car. Sitting in the parking lot at the small airfield, he dialed Zoe's number.

"I'm going to block you," she said upon answering.

"Then I'm glad you answered this one last call," Cord replied smoothly. "I'm also hoping you'll agree to see me one last time."

He heard the weight of her sigh through the phone.

"Cord, really, stop flogging a dead horse. We can't work. You know we can't, and you know damn well why. Nothing's going to change that."

"One last time, Zoe. Please. We owe it to ourselves," he cajoled her.

"I thought the last time was the last," she answered.

He could tell by her tone she was thinking about it.

"I promise you, this will be the last time I bother you. No more gifts, no more calls, no more touching you—"

"All right!" she interrupted in a fierce whisper. "You win. One last time. When?"

"Can you manage a few hours off today? Say I pick you up at your apartment about two?"

"Cord—"

"Please," he all but begged. "Just this one *last* time, Zoe."

He held his breath as she hesitated.

"Fine, pick me up at two. I'll be ready."

She severed the call before he could say another word, but inside he felt his heart begin to beat again and felt the air around him refill his lungs. He'd never wanted anything as much as he wanted the rest of today to go right.

Zoe paced her living room, waiting for the buzz from security downstairs to say Cord had arrived. She'd left explicit instructions for him not to be let up to her apartment. If she was being totally honest with herself, she didn't know if she could trust herself around him. Since their last night together she'd missed him with a physical ache that no amount of overtime could assuage.

Her apartment phone buzzed, making her flinch. She picked up the receiver.

"Your guest has arrived, Ms. Warren."

"Thank you. Tell him I'll be right down."

Her heart was fluttering in her chest as she entered the elevator to head to the lobby. She clenched her hands into fists and deliberately relaxed each finger in turn, telling herself this reaction was ridiculous. This was their final meeting. The last goodbye. She felt a twist of sorrow deep inside her and pushed it ruthlessly away. This was what she wanted. Closure. An end to the restless nights and the unexpected and totally unbidden memories that flooded her mind at the most inopportune moments. An end to seeing a dark head on a tall, rangy body everywhere she went and wondering if it was him.

And then the elevator doors were sliding open and her eyes were searching for that figure that never seemed far from the periphery of her thoughts. The second her gaze alighted on him, she felt his presence with a physical impact that robbed her of breath and made a hot flush of need rise slowly through her body. She tugged at the front of her leather jacket and strode toward him as if she were totally in control and not at all feeling like she was on the verge of wrapping her arms around him, absorbing him—everything from his heat to his breath to the flavor of him—so she could tuck it away forever.

She came to an abrupt halt about three feet away. He gave her a nod.

"Thanks for making time for me today. I know it probably wasn't easy, especially at such short notice, but I want you to know I appreciate it. Shall we go?"

Wow, heavy on the formal, she noted as he gestured for her to precede him from the building. Not even an attempt to take her hand or kiss her? What was with that, and why the heck was she so upset about it, anyway? It was what she wanted, wasn't it? She came to a stop on the sidewalk and felt him come up behind her, stopping mere inches from her body. She sensed everything about him with a heightened awareness that was going to drive her absolutely crazy if she didn't wrestle it under control.

"Where to?" she asked, fighting to keep the tremor from her voice. Inside, her nerves skittered as he drew up beside her.

"My car." He gestured to the nondescript sedan parked in the visitor's area.

She saw the lights flash as he unlocked it and then stepped forward as he held open the passenger door. She got in, glancing at him as she settled into the seat. He hadn't smiled yet, not so much as a glimmer. That wasn't like him, and the firm set to his jaw made her nervous. This was ridiculous, she told herself. She knew this man, intimately, she reminded herself with a curl of desire licking its way through her body. Whatever he had planned for her, she had nothing to fear except maybe the loss of her own self-control.

And maybe that was what she feared most. She knew he affected her on levels she had never experienced with any of her previous lovers. Heck, even that word—*lover*—was enough to make her entire body tighten in a wave of lust so intense it almost made her cry out.

Cord settled into the driver's seat and started up the vehicle.

"How've you been?" she asked, desperate to break the silence that filled the car so awkwardly.

"Not great. You?"

She sighed. So much for that gambit. "Same," she answered and fell silent again, at a total loss for words.

What did you say to a man whose very presence turned you into a melting puddle of mush, desperate for his touch and to touch him in return? A man you'd turned away from your bed, your life. A man whose absence left a gaping hole in every single day. She turned her head and stared out at the road, watching as they headed out of the city.

"Where are you taking me?" she asked, her nerves stretched to breaking point.

"Airfield."

"What's with the short answers?" she demanded, letting her anger begin to rise in the vain hope it would quell the insecurity that plagued her.

"I'm saving myself," he answered shortly.

"For what?"

He took his eyes from the road ahead and flung her a searing glance. "You'll find out."

"What if I don't want to find out?" she said, taking refuge in belligerence.

This time it was his turn to sigh. "Zoe, just be patient, okay? You granted me this time, and I promise you it won't tax or harm you in any way. For now, we're headed to the airfield. What I want to show you is a short way from town, but I want you to see it from the air, rather than the ground."

"Fine." She crossed her arms over her. "Thank you for at least telling me that much."

She didn't have to wait much longer. At the airfield, Cord pulled into a restricted zone and swiped a card at the security gate before driving alongside the tarmac to where she recognized his helicopter sitting just inside a hangar. Questions tumbled through her mind, but she resolved to hold her tongue as they walked to the chopper, and he dragged it to the helipad and prepped it for takeoff.

Before she knew it, she was feeling that delicious lurch in her stomach as they took to the air. She loved the sensation. The only thing better was sex, and she sure as heck wasn't going to go there. Not when she was doing her level best to remind herself of all the reasons why she and Cord would never work. She began to list them in her mind, taking strength from each one. He lived too far away. He hated her job. He hated the fact she carried a gun. He was traditional and wanted to take care of her, when she was eminently capable of caring for herself. He… Her thoughts trailed off. Okay, so there were four reasons, but they were important enough to be deal breakers as far as she was concerned.

Her headset crackled to life.

"Look down there, to your left."

Zoe did as he suggested. "Looks like a ranch."

"It's a goat ranch. Angora, mostly."

"And the reason you're showing me this is…?"

"It's mine."

She swiveled to face him. "It's yours? But what about your spread in Royal? Who's going to look after that?"

"My parents, and some extra hands."

"But why?"

"Well, you remember the cheese, right?"

"Sure, it was delicious."

"I've been wanting to diversify for a long time, but Dad's a cattleman through and through. So we had an honest talk. Turned out he wasn't enjoying retirement but didn't want to step on my toes by coming back home."

"But why not run the goats on your existing family property, or buy more land closer to home?"

"Because you're not there."

His words hung in the air between them.

"But—" She started to protest, but he cut her off.

"Just hear me out. I can do what I want to do anywhere, especially now that I'm no longer tied to the family spread. Sure, I'll help Dad when necessary, but I don't have to live there."

"But your family, your history. That ranch is every-thing to you, isn't it?"

"It's not you."

Zoe felt her stomach dip again as he took the chopper down and settled it in an empty field at the top of a rise. Once he'd shut down the engine, they alighted from the chopper, and Zoe stomped after Cord as he moved away from the machine to where there was a great vantage point over the land they'd flown over.

"What do you mean, it's not me?" she demanded, pok-ing him in the chest for good measure.

"Exactly what I said. I've fallen for you, Detective. You have my heart in your custody, and that's where it's going to be for the rest of my life."

"You can't say that. You barely know me," Zoe pro-tested, fear threatening to choke her.

This was all too intense. This was supposed to be good-bye, and here he was, telling her he'd walked off his fam-ily's land and bought a ranch close to Houston so he could be nearer to her. Who did that? What craziness had crawled into his brain?

"That's true, but what I do know is that you're a prickly pear with a soft inside. You're diligent in your work, you're a fierce advocate for the underdog, whether they're a good person or not. I know you have the softest lips of any woman I've ever met and that you make love as fiercely as you defend your independence."

"That doesn't tell me why you did this. I made it clear we had no future. I'm not giving up my work to set up house with any man."

"I'm not asking you to give up work, Zoe. I'm asking you for a chance at a future together. I love you."

All the air left her lungs in a massive whoosh. There it was. Those three words. Words she'd craved and yet dreaded at the same time. Words that bound and trapped. She started to shake her head, but Cord closed the distance between them and caught her by her shoulders, forcing her to look at him.

"I love you, Zoe Warren. I want to make a future with you, if you'll let me."

"No," she whispered. "I can't. You want all the things I can't give you. My career is everything to me. You want a family, you want a stay-at-home wife who'll raise your kids and work alongside you on the ranch. I'm not that woman."

"Oh, Zoe, don't be scared. Yeah, I thought I wanted those things. But most of all I just want you. I'd be happy if we never had a family, as long as I knew you loved me and could live here with me. The commute isn't so far into Houston from here. We could make a future together."

"I can't do it, Cord," she said as her eyes glazed with tears. "You hate my job and everything related to it. Yes, it can be dangerous. Yes, my life can be on the line. But I have to keep doing this. Eventually, you'd ask me to give it up. I know you would. Eventually, you'd want to have kids. I don't know if that's ever going to be on my radar. I can't do that to you. I carry a badge and a gun pretty much every day of my life. It's who I am."

"And that's who I love. Don't you see? I *want* to make compromises so we can be together. What we have is incredible and special, and we deserve to be happy together. Please, Zoe, at least give us a chance."

Zoe continued to shake her head. "No, it'll never work. Eventually you'd expect me to change, and I won't do that."

"Or maybe it's just that you're too scared to try," he challenged her. "Too scared to reach for what you know is good. Too scared to be seen as anything but bulletproof

Detective Warren, who feels no emotions but always gets her man. Trouble is, Zoe, your man is standing right here in front of you, but you're too scared to take a chance on me."

"Maybe you're right, but that's who and what I am," she said, lifting her chin and staring him straight in the eyes. "Take me back. It's over, Cord."

Fifteen

Even as she said the words, it was as if a .45-caliber hollow-nose bullet tore through her heart. Cord just continued to look at her, as if unable to believe she was still saying no to what he offered. How could he not see how impossible it was? Sure, she could commute to work from here, maybe even keep her apartment in town for those times she pulled an all-nighter, but she was certain he still hoped that eventually she'd leave her work, put aside the potential danger, and settle down and play happy family. And even if she did that, she knew eventually she'd come to hate it—maybe even hate him. No, it was easier to stand strong, to ignore the allure of what he offered and to let him walk away.

As they transferred from the aircraft to his rental car, she saw him grab a parcel and stow it behind the driver's seat. It was only when they got to her apartment building and she opened her door to get out that he reached for it again.

"Hang on a second," he said, his voice gruff with emotion. "I bought this for you. You should have it. My last gift to you, okay?"

She didn't trust herself to speak. His voice was so desolate, so devoid of hope or joy, and it scored her heart into a million pieces to know she'd done this to him. She accepted the parcel from him and got out of the car, closing the door behind her and walking as quickly as she could back into the lobby. She punched the elevator button with a shaking finger and rode the car up to her floor, her eyes blurring with unshed tears.

When she let herself into her apartment, she gave in to the hideous pain that had begun back at Cord's new ranch and grown in intensity each time she'd said no to him. Her legs buckled and she knelt on the floor of her entrance hall and wept as she'd never wept before.

Once the first wave of the emotional storm had passed, Zoe realized she was still holding the parcel Cord had given her. She plucked at the tape and tore the paper away from a case. One she identified immediately. With shaking fingers, she opened the snaps on the case to expose the brand-new SIG Sauer handgun inside. She recognized the model because it was one she'd been planning to upgrade to. With its reduced-reach trigger and one-piece modular grip, it was a far more comfortable weapon for her to use, when she was forced to.

But it wasn't the gun that made her begin trembling all over again. It was the fact that he'd bought it for her. She knew how much he hated weapons and why. But he'd gone out and bought her the exact model she was planning to buy for herself. More than anything he'd said as he'd tried to persuade her at the new ranch, this spoke volumes as to just how far he was prepared to compromise to have her in his world.

Could she even dare to hope that they stood a chance? That he'd meant exactly what he'd said back there? That they could make a future together? The enormity of what he'd done, of the things he'd said back at the new ranch rained down on her like giant hailstones. She'd been such an idiot. Caught up in her rut of fierce independence, she hadn't stopped to see that she was ignoring everything her heart was begging for. Everything she'd always told herself she'd make time for when the time was right. But when would that time be if she never allowed the love of a decent and good man into her life? If she threw up walls at every opportunity? If all she ever did was take and give nothing back in return? She had to make this right.

Zoe was up on her feet in seconds, and after shoving the new pistol into her gun safe, she grabbed her car keys and headed down to the parking garage. But where would she go? The airfield? What if, by the time she got there, he'd taken off again? The new ranch? Had he even taken possession of it yet? And what if he was flying back to Royal? She had a responsibility to her job to turn up tomorrow. But wasn't Cord more important? For the first time in her life, she put the needs of someone else ahead of her job. She'd start with the airfield, then head out to the ranch, if she could find it on a map. Hell, she was a detective. If she couldn't find an address with the resources available to her, she may as well hand in her badge right now.

And if he wasn't at either place? What then? She started her car and peeled out of the parking garage, driven by a desperate sense of urgency. She'd tackle that when she'd exhausted her local resources, she decided. But one way or another, she would find him.

This wasn't how it was meant to turn out, Cord thought after he'd handed in the rental car and taken a cab to the airfield. He prepped the Robinson for takeoff automatically, trying to ignore the deep sense of loss that had settled inside him. He'd put everything on the line and it had still turned to dust in the wind. All his hopes, all his dreams, shattered. He knew he couldn't do this again. Couldn't put his life and his heart on the line a third time. This was it. The thought of telling his parents and Abuelita that he'd failed was a bitter taste in his mouth. He should have known better than to trust in love again.

The sound of tires screeching to a halt behind the security fencing to the airfield caught his attention and made him look up from his preparations. Then there was the sound of a woman's voice, shouting—no, pleading—with the guy at the security gate. Cord walked to where he could see what all the fuss was about. As he did so, recognition dawned and with it an ember of hope stirred in his chest.

"It's okay," he called out. "She's with me."

"Sir, you know this is an operational airfield. We can't just let people in all over the place."

"I understand. My apologies."

Cord planted his feet firmly on the ground and watched as Zoe pushed past the guard and through the gate, actually running toward him with a look of desperation on her face that fanned that ember to a warm glow. Even so, he didn't plan to make this easy. She'd crushed him. If she truly was back for him, as hard as it would be, he might actually let her fight for it.

"You haven't left yet," she said breathlessly as she drew up in front of him.

"Your powers of observation are on point, as always, Detective," he drawled, not letting an ounce of the emotions that crashed through him surface in the sound of his voice.

"I need to talk to you."

"I thought we were all talked out."

She slid her sunglasses off her face, and he was shocked to see the ravaging evidence of tears there. Zoe was one tough nut. He'd never have expected tears from her. Not in a million years. His every instinct urged him forward, to take her into his arms, to console her and make everything right, but instead he locked his knees and stood firm right where he was.

"Cord, I'm sorry," she started. "I made a stupid mistake."

He kept his peace, not trusting himself to speak.

"Look," she continued, "can we go somewhere a little less out in the open?"

"Nope."

"You want me to do this here?"

"Yup."

"Fine, then." She chewed her lower lip for a second. "I want another chance. I want to take you up on your offer. I want to tell you I was a stupid, prideful, frightened fool who thought she knew what she wanted. But when I walked away from you," she admitted, "I realized how much I really wanted you after all. I'm sorry, Cord. I love you. I guess I was fighting it because it all happened so damn fast. Heck, a few weeks ago I was prepared to arrest you for obstruction and now I want to spend the rest of my life with you."

Every cell in Cord's body shuddered as the impact of her words sank in.

"The rest of your life, you say?" he finally managed to enunciate, hardly daring to believe her words.

"Forever, Cord. I know a love like this doesn't come along often. My parents have it. My brothers have it. I want it, too, with you."

"So, um, marriage? And kids?"

"Yes, marriage and kids…eventually."

He nodded and looked away to the distance so she wouldn't immediately see the gathering moisture in his eyes as the realization of his dreams began to take shape again.

"Today wasn't easy for me," Cord said carefully, still not looking at her. "The last woman I wanted to spend a future with died in the line of duty. The same duty you take on every day you roll up to work."

"I understand that," Zoe said, taking a step closer and reaching out with both hands to turn his face toward hers. "I promise you that I will always do my level best to be as safe as I can possibly be. Beyond that, I have to trust my fellow officers to do their jobs to the best of their abilities, too. You can live with that?"

He allowed his gaze to meet and mesh with hers. "I have to, if I want you in my life, and I do want you, Zoe. I want to build a family with you, the way our parents did with us. I want to grow old with you. I know it's never going to be an easy ride—we're both too strong willed for that. I could never make a life with a biddable woman, anyway. I love your sass, your determination, your strength. Quite simply, I love you."

"Then you'll forgive me for being an idiot this afternoon? For nearly crushing us forever?"

"You may need to make that up to me," he said with a slow, teasing grin beginning to wreath his mouth. "For quite some time."

"I'll do anything you want. Come home with me now. We can make plans."

"Plans?"

"Well, after we…y'know."

"So you liked the gun, then, huh?"

"I love the gun, Cord, but even more than that, I love

what it symbolizes between you and me. And, Cord, I love you even more."

He grabbed her then and kissed her with all the pent-up hope and joy and relief and love that had surged through him the second he'd identified her behind the security gate. And he knew that while they might weather some storms, they'd do it together—stronger for all they'd fought for, better for having each other.

Epilogue

The hot breath of the police was a tangible sensation down my neck. They were getting closer and it was making me nervous. My hands kept sweating, I'd lost weight, my hair was falling out. Thank God no one had noticed yet. I was holding it together when it counted—just.

This craziness wasn't me. It wasn't my fault. I had no choice. Surely they'd see that, wouldn't they? The Sterlings and the Currins, they were the ones to blame. They had everything, and they took even more—the land that should have been my father's, the land that Ryder Currin had coerced out of Harrington York and that he'd made his fortune on.

I thought I'd properly put a spoke in Currin's relationship with Angela. The golden child. The woman with everything. Her daddy's right hand. None of them deserved happiness. Not at my expense.

And then there was that bitch cop who kept poking and

prodding where she shouldn't. It made me laugh when I heard she'd gone out of town on some goose chase to Royal when I'd been right under her nose all along. But she was back now, and more determined than ever.

I had to find my baby before they found out it was me. My child was the only thing keeping me going now. But I'd never find her if I was in prison. Please, don't let me lose my last chance to find my child, to hold her, to love her. To put right the wrongs of eighteen years ago.

Ryder Currin watched as Willem Inwood entered the boardroom and settled at the table with his lawyer by his side. Slimy bastard. He still couldn't believe that this feeble excuse for an executive had abused Ryder's staff and pretty much gotten away with it. And to think it was Ryder who'd given Inwood every opportunity to get ahead at Currin Oil. He'd believed the man to be loyal. The discovery that Inwood was the complete opposite had left a nasty bitter taste in his mouth.

He stared at Inwood, determined not to be the first to speak, taking in the slightly less-than-perfect dark auburn hair, the lanky frame and the dark brown eyes hidden behind his wire-framed glasses.

Ryder had never understood why a man such as Inwood, as insecure as he'd turned out to be, had to turn that insecurity on to his subordinates, instead of learning and growing. Inwood had been a complete failure as an executive on his payroll and it irked Ryder greatly that he hadn't noticed sooner and thereby had a chance to minimize the damage Inwood had wrought.

Inwood tugged at the tie at his collar and stretched his neck. It gave Ryder no small amount of pleasure to see the other man was uncomfortable in his presence. Inwood cast a glance at his lawyer, who nodded as if encouraging him to speak. *Great*, Ryder thought, *let the show begin.*

"I asked you to meet me here today to apologize for my actions. I should never have rekindled the rumors that you had an affair with Tamara Perry, and I apologize for the way I conducted myself while working for you."

"Is that so?" Ryder drawled. "Strange that you didn't seem to think that necessary when I fired you. Nor did you seem to think it necessary when you were haranguing staff and forcing them to falsify paperwork a couple of months ago when it became clear you were incapable of performing your duties properly, let alone adequately."

Hot color flushed the man's face, and his lips twisted into a feral grimace, showing him for the weasel he truly was.

"Look, I didn't need to come here today and put up with your insults!"

His lawyer leaned across and whispered urgently into his ear. To Ryder's surprise, Inwood settled down in his seat.

"I came here to clear the air. I've said I'm sorry. I didn't mean for any of this to go this far. Whether you accept that or not is up to you. But I also need to make something absolutely clear. I didn't kill Vincent Hamm. I never even met the guy. My lawyer will present you with the results of a polygraph that I voluntarily took to prove my innocence."

Ryder watched as the lawyer removed a sheaf of papers from the folder in front of him and slid it across the table. He picked up the data and scanned it quickly before reading the summary at the end.

"So this proves you didn't kill Hamm. But I have a sneaky feeling you know who did, don't you?" Ryder pressed.

Inwood's face paled. The red hue that had suffused his skin earlier now faded to a sickly gray. He shook his head.

"No, you've got it all wrong. In fact—" he pushed up from his chair and stood facing Ryder "—you can go to hell. I'd never give up my—"

Inwood closed his mouth with a snap, as if realizing that he was on the verge of saying something incriminating.

"You'd never give up your what?" Ryder prompted.

Inwood just shook his head and turned for the door. As it slammed behind him and his lawyer, who'd scurried out after him, Ryder leaned back in his chair and whistled softly through his lips. What was it that Inwood had been on the verge of saying? Was it a *who* or a *what* that he would never give up? One thing was for certain—Ryder would soon find out.

* * * * *

LET'S TALK

Romance

For exclusive extracts, competitions
and special offers, find us online:

f facebook.com/millsandboon

⌾ @millsandboonuk

🐦 @millsandboon

Or get in touch on 0844 844 1351*

For all the latest titles coming soon,
visit millsandboon.co.uk/nextmonth